Then the horror began.

The body of the woman Libby had been found first, in the kitchen of Gus's house. She had been stabbed with a kitchen knife.

Her brother Robert had also been stabbed, twice, but had somehow crawled out of the house and across the yard to the gill, leaving a trail of blood as he went. He had been found lying face down in the stream, the knife still in his back, arms outstretched. Just beyond his reach, in the water, tangled in the overgrowth on the edge, the infant's body was found, dead from either a crushed skull or drowning, they didn't know yet, lying partially in, partially out of a red toy boat.

". . . Sort of a toy dory, you know, a pretty thing."

Hawley was watching my reaction, and made a quick gesture to his sergeant when I looked as though I was going to faint. I know I reeled for a moment. I could feel the color and the warmth drain from me, as though the life was flooding out of me into the floor. Then the reaction came in its opposite form, and a scream of rage and horror was in my throat choking me to be let out.

CEREMONY OF INNOCENCE

S.F.X. DEAN

CEREMONY OF INNOCENCE

TOR

A TOM DOHERTY ASSOCIATES BOOK

CEREMONY OF INNOCENCE

Copyright © 1984 by S.F.X. Dean

Reprinted by arrangement with Walker and Company

First Tor printing: January 1987

A TOR Book

Published by Tom Doherty Associates, Inc.
49 West 24 Street
New York, N.Y. 10010

ISBN: 0-812-50186-1
CAN. ED.: 0-812-50187-X

Library of Congress Catalog Card Number: 83-40403

Printed in the United States of America

0   9   8   7   6   5   4   3   2   1

For

Our Gang
eight of a kind
all different

*"The blood-dimmed tide is loosed, and everywhere
The ceremony of innocence is drowned . . .*

Surely some revelation is at hand"

—W.B. Yeats

Devon & Cornwall
POLICE

MURDER
APPEAL

On Sunday 24th May 1981
Elizabeth Grandisson, Robert Grandisson and Richard Van Duren were murdered at the home of Austin and Susan Van Duren, a detached house in Lower Mill Lane, Raleigh's Gill.

Were **you** in this **area** between **8am** and 1 PM on that day?

Did you see anything suspicious, or anyone acting suspiciously?

Has a stranger called at your home?

If you have any information, however insignificant it might seem contact the police

'PHONE: EXMOUTH 4651

1

AT THE END of it, standing for a final time in the Raleigh's Cask drinking a pint of the good local bitter, I felt the anger in me ebb away to sadness. The anger itself had persisted as the ebb of rage, and the rage had exhausted me and turned my grief to bitterness, and my honest mourning to the raw energy that drives vengeance.

I had come to this tiny English coastal village for a sabbatical respite from the horrors of what had happened to my personal life back home in Massachusetts. Now, drinking a valedictory pint just this short time later, I wondered where I might find peace if I had not found it here. Peace, instead of murder and betrayal and the implacable evil of an obsession calling itself idealism, but which excludes mercy even for those who are wholly innocent.

Looking back, it is so clear how events ten thousand miles and fifty years apart had found their pattern and their final awful significance in this place now.

Raleighston was not the place I had expected to be living when I had come to England in late April, but my original destination, Ottery St. Mary, had proven inhospitable.

I had flown out of Boston just ahead of a late season nor'easter and into London behind a cleansing cold front that left the sky and the old city bright. I was lavishly attended on the flight, the cabin crew made pleasant by my first-class ticket, a courtesy arranged by Mary Dowd, of all people. Heathrow, for once in April, was unstruck by its service unions.

An Airbus service, something new to me, took me to Paddington direct and immediately out to Exeter on one of the fast intercity trains. All blessedly easy and quick. Jet lag had never dissipated so gently. In spite of my feeling that my lucky streak had to stop when I encountered local transportation, I managed an easy cab hire with a silent, skillful driver who got me the dozen miles to Ottery St. Mary in twenty minutes.

Months earlier, I had reserved for myself by mail a small self-serve cottage on the grounds of an old Regency estate that had been turned into holiday accommodations. I had paid in advance for a month, of which two weeks had already passed while I was tying up loose ends back home. It had not occurred to me that my tardiness had been construed as a permanent change of plans by my putative landlady.

I paid off the taciturn, toothless elder who had driven me and stood surveying my new digs with satisfaction, my two canvas bags at my feet. When you hire a place you know only from a picture and a description in a brochure, you always run all the risks attending pig-in-a-poke purchases. But my recognizable temporary home, Brown Cottage, situated at an angle to the road facing a tiny stream, its lawn carpeted to the door with yellow daffodils, was reassuring.

The stout woman standing at the front door with her fists on her hips bawling a name that sounded like "Ree-chard," and who must be my landlady, was not reassuring. Nor was she my landlady, as it turned out. Ten minutes of baffling conversation between us, with me assuming the house was mine and she assuming I was a rapist or a vandal claiming to be an American professor of literature, come to kidnap her Reechard, revealed that this noisy person was the current tenant of my house.

"But, my dear madam, I paid a month's rent for this house."

"That's not my concern, is it? I paid, is all I know, and I'm here. Me and my Reechard. There's no use you standing there as if you're going to get inside, because you're not."

"Where does the landlady live?"

"Who might that be?"

"The owner, then."

"Owner's off in Honiton, isn't he?" She seemed delighted

2

at this thrust, which clearly revealed me to her as even more of an imposter.

"The manager then." In one more sentence I would be yelling.

"Mrs. Gilbert is it you want?"

"Yes, she'll do. Where is she?"

"I dunno if she's in." She started to shut the door, but was stopped by the appearance of a boy of about nine, apparently the errant Richard. Her blood-curdling shriek caused him to grimace and look down at the sodden shoes she was pointing to.

"You've been in the stree-um, haven't you, you naughty disobedient little bastard, haven't you?" She grabbed him to her pendulous bosom, which hung comfortably about her waist for such purposes, and simultaneously hugged, berated, and clouted him. "I thought this man had kidnapped you and done away with you, did you know that? Did you?"

The boy simply howled and blubbered.

I picked up my bags and walked dazedly up the dirt path past what I was beginning to think was not, after all, my cottage. Thirty yards off the road, partially screened by a glossy hedge of ivy at its corner, was a more imposing structure that appeared to be a converted coachhouse of some kind, painted pink except for its four white front doors. From the first door came a thin woman in a blue cardigan, looking at me mildly over the upper edge of her glasses.

"Are you Mrs. Gilbert?"

"Yes. Are you looking for a flat?"

"I'm Professor Neil Kelly." She betrayed no emotion on hearing that fact. "From the United States." Nor that one. "I rented the Brown Cottage for three months." Light seemed to be dawning. "I sent you a check for a month, starting April fifteenth. Weeks ago." Her eyes widened. "There is a woman and a child living in my cottage."

She put her hand to her mouth and took it away. "I heard you were in prison."

"Well, then, I've escaped, haven't I?" It was a grim

3

pleasantry, intended to thaw my own exasperation and her slow wits, but it obviously only served to frighten her out of the few wits she had.

"Well, then, you can't stay here, can you? If you're wanted by the police, it would be my duty to tell them you're here and come and get you, wouldn't it?" She had clumsy, cheap false teeth; she leered at me with them.

"It would be, yes. If I had. Look, that was a joke. Whoever told you I was in prison made a mistake."

She straightened her glasses and looked at me sideways through them. They appeared to blind her. "My sister told me. In a letter."

"Does your sister know me, or I her?"

"She lives in Oldhampton, Massachusetts, same as you. Lived there for ten years. Works at the college. She was the one suggested we advertise in that magazine. She's married to campus police. Should know."

I waited, as patiently as encroaching fatigue permitted, for her explanation to sputter itself out to its full length. Apparently my progress had been fully attended by the Gilbert family espionage apparatus ever since I had left my campus and hometown in the company of an FBI agent the first week in April. I had not gone to prison, but to the hospital bedside of an old and loved friend who had been horribly injured and whose husband had been killed. The complexities of the case had taken me to Santa Fe, New Mexico, then, instead of to Devon, England, and had involved me with both the FBI and the CIA. God knows what local gossip had made of it all, but I was hearing part of it now, at least.

Her glasses slipped down her long nose again, and she resumed studying me over their rims. "My sister said it was in the papers about you being a spy."

I sighed; this woman had hold of an idea she obviously cherished. No recitation of facts by me, exonerating myself from all charges, would ever match whatever juicy tabloid version of my crimes her sister in Oldhampton had provided in advance of my coming.

4

"I sent you a check for four hundred dollars. I am not a criminal. I am a tired teacher who needs to rest and who wants to write a book about a seventeenth-century English poet."

"Samuel Taylor Coleridge," she snapped like a contestant on a game show, hungry for the ticket for two to Acapulco. Or at least for the videorecorder.

"Mrs. Gilbert, if your sister told you that I'm interested in Samuel Coleridge, she was wrong about that, too. Besides, he is from the wrong century."

"Seventeen seventy-two to eighteen thirty-four," she barked.

"Four hundred dollars!" I roared back at her. Sometimes one must speak to landladies, especially English landladies, in their own vernacular. If it was to be a duel of facts, I wanted to fight with relevant ones.

"He was born right here in this village, you know, so don't pretend you don't. If you are a professor," she added slyly above the glasses.

"I am in this village now, and I have paid good money for the use of that cottage, and you have rented it to that woman and that dirty kid with muddy shoes who has been walking in your creek and who is probably at this moment walking with those same shoes all over your gold-colored close carpeting."

It was a cruel stroke. Her mouth fell open. "He didn't ever."

"Who knows? *I* wouldn't have!" This was insane. "Why did you rent my cottage to someone else? I want my check back."

"Well." She looked hurt and her lip trembled and her eyes grew watery. "You didn't arrive when you said. And my sister Rose said you were in jail out west for being a spy. And Mrs. Will Banky and Richard came along and wanted it bad, and what would you have done? I did what I thought was right. I'm only a woman trying to make a go of this place by myself. *He* doesn't care." She sniffed viciously. "Him off in Honiton running his garage business and counting the money I earn for him here, managing and caretaking and sorting out every stranger and foreigner who wants to come in here." The recitation of her tragedy was too much for her. She brimmed over and wept into the glasses, rummaging blindly in her cardigan pockets for tissues, which she finally produced and swabbed her face and spectacles with.

You must never melt before such performances. They come only after years of practice, and their purpose is to rout the tenderhearted in a confusion of pity and embarrassment. You must demand your money even more loudly. This I did.

"Oh, I still have your check." She sniffed and waved away my most pressing concern with irritating offhandedness. "I was waiting for Rose to tell me if I could cash it or if the American police would come after me if I did." She pointed to the ground I stood on. "You stay there, if you please, and I'll get your check for you." She disappeared into a chintz and varnished-pine interior. I shuddered with the sudden realization of what the interior of Brown Cottage might be like if this female had been the perpetrator of its decoration.

Mrs. Gilbert appeared clutching a blue check to her chest and looked at me first over, then sideways through her glasses. "Do you have proper identification?"

Having been abused for twenty minutes in my own right, this seemed gratuitous, but I bit back any further reply and produced my billfold and extracted my own faculty ID. She read the small plastic card with slow, skeptical interest.

"Well, I suppose." She handed it back to me. "I find it a little surprising, Professor, that you never heard of Samuel Taylor Coleridge. He's quite famous, you understand."

I put my hand out for the check and got it. "Few English people know, Mrs. Gilbert, that Samuel Taylor Coleridge and William Wordsworth's sister Dorothy were one and the same person, and not actually born in this village at all."

I tipped my hat and picked up my bags and walked off. My jet lag had finally caught up with me. Why else was I lying spitefully to this poor soul behind me? I almost turned to apologize.

"One paper said you were blown up by a bomb," she cried brokenly after me.

I did not have the faintest idea where I was going, but I did not stop. What she had said was only true in part.

2

OTTERY ST. MARY had been a thriving village before William the Conqueror did in the Saxons, but its great age came after. Its church, a near miniature of the Exeter Cathedral, is a marvel of architectural judgment and a near miracle of Victorian restoration, spared as it was the decorative excesses which constituted the higher taste of that awful time.

That church, St. Mary's, was the symbol of what had brought me back here in the first place. In its delicate Lady Chapel, with its stone screen and fourteenth-century benches, Georgia and I had been married some thirty years before. Ottery St. Mary had been her native place, and her parents had lived here until their deaths. I had come here not only to read the sermons of John Donne and to try to understand the poet who became the priest, but to find my own spirit's adult roots, the beginnings of my responsible manhood and the calm places of memory that might heal my confusion.

A cheerful and polite teenager who looked like one of my own students—well, one of the politer ones—back at Old Hampton College stopped his van and leaned out to ask me with some concern if he could give me a lift. I suppose it was my standing beside the road with my luggage looking lost that suggested the idea to him.

"There's no coach along here, you know," he added.

"That's very kind of you. I don't really know yet where I'm going. To an inn, I suppose."

"You're American." His brightening surprise made me feel both exotic and welcome, neither a common feeling in the season for Yank tourists in Devon. "My father was an American, hop in."

I wasn't sure of the sequitur, but I heaved my bags into

the back of his tidy van next to a dozen huge rolls of cloth and climbed in beside him.

His name was Jeremy. Like my students, he apparently had no last name. If I was in any doubt about where to go next, Jeremy was not.

"They throw you out of there? You look pretty angry."

"It's a long, boring story, Jeremy. But I do need a place to stay tonight and a place to eat. I've been awake for just about twenty-four hours, and it's catching up with me."

"No sweat." He grinned at the Americanism. "I'm going down to Sidmouth with these rolls of fabric, and there's a grand place just a mile or so down here. A famous old place, but with all mod. cons. The people who run it are great and the food's terrific. Do try the ossobuco." He made the recommendation lightly, but stayed attentive for my reaction, too.

"My, my. You seem to know it well."

"I worked there busing and like that for a year. My father was the chef there once. He used to be a cook in the American army—not all army cooks are hacks, y'know—but he stayed here after he got pensioned, and then he ran a little restaurant in Lyme Regis until he died. I'm going to be a cook, a chef eventually. First I have to get some money together and go to a good school. In France, I hope."

He was an altogether pleasant, uncomplaining, and hopeful young man, and he reeled off his whole life history on an army base and his recipe for leek pie, which he called by its Cornish name, Likky pie, like someone talking about very serious matters indeed.

"The Cornish saints praised Likky pie, you know," he assured me, "but only if it was made with eggs and a double crust. To be preferred to ambrosia, they said."

He chatted pleasantly all through unloading my bags for me at the inn where he pulled up. He shook my hand amiably and wished me a nice holiday. I was willing to assume that any place he recommended had a lot going for it, and went in confidently.

The Fisherman Inn was as good as Jeremy had promised. I was to discover later that the ossobuco was, too. My room

9

was plain and cheery with light, and obviously kept clean by people who thought cleanliness as important as good taste. I looked out over the green fields to the west, where black-and-white cattle were standing, and began at last to feel the peace I had come to Devon for. That or the final arrival of total exhaustion. A thin mist was beginning to drizzle over the trees.

An hour later, mellowed by a bath and a nap, I went down to the Salmon Bar, where the firelight burned a hundredfold in the hammered copper on the walls. I ordered a mug of scrumpy, the local vinegary cider my palate still remembered. I sat by myself along the side wall, content to observe the few other guests at this early hour and to let the reality of my present situation sink in, blinking for a moment the fact that I'd have to go out hunting a new place tomorrow.

Then Gus Van Duren came through the door and my easy plans for writing and loafing changed dramatically, although neither he nor I knew then that they would.

Scientists understand now just how it is that a migrating creature—a salmon, for example—can move out of the stream in which he is spawned, spend a career out in the Atlantic, then unerringly home back in on the exact river, and its exact tributary, and that tributary's precise rill, to return to the spot of his birth. Salmon, eels, migrating birds, are all born with a map that they must follow. It isn't that they have a map of their world in their brain; each has a map of that world *for* a brain. That map is global, and is actually a hologram.

The most interesting thing about a hologram—one of those three-dimensional pictures of something produced in a laboratory by laser beams—is that you make a photographic plate, then a holograph, of it. Then, if you break that in half, you get two whole pictures. If you break each half of the print in half, you get four whole pictures. If you break it a thousand times, each fragment will be a whole copy of the original, like the image on each facet of a housefly's eye. It is less a portrait of something than a printed, in-depth memory of the whole thing. Some scientists think that the human brain is essentially holographic, that we have in our heads what amounts to a memory of the whole universe that involves us—a global map of our own humanness, which we must follow to our destiny.

Plato believed something not very different, and so did St. Augustine, the greatest philosopher among the Church Fathers. It is a metaphor that accounts for Jung's "collective unconscious" and for the Hindu concept of rebirth, and a lot more.

For some of us the map is exact and accessible for only a small space: the neighborhood of our childhood, for example, or the geography of the first house we ever lived in. These places will recur forever in our dreams because they are a deeply etched background for everything else we experience in our lives, no matter how far we travel from them. Dublin was Joyce's map; the Mississippi was Mark Twain's. The mind migrates back for the soul's reasons; those reasons become our fate.

Early life, early dreads, first hatreds, first friendships are never forgotten. They become the global models against which all later enmities or friendships are measured or felt.

Gus Van Duren became my friend when we were both seven, two navy brats in China. His father was a British captain acting as naval attaché in their embassy, and mine was an American commander assigned to a dead-end job in the American embassy.

Few of the officers' families were Catholic, so Gus and I were thrown together simply by finding ourselves the only two foreigners in the First Communion class at the cathedral. We were both bookish rather than athletic, and were both to become fairly nimble in the Chinese language. If anything, that increased our distance from a lot of the other embassy brats; Chinese was the language of the servants, and only officers with responsibilities requiring linguistic facility were expected to learn it.

Gus's grandfather had been a scoundrel and so had mine, and we gleefully swapped stories that our respective families were trying to suppress. His had abandoned the responsibilities of managing a huge family estate south of Albany, New York ("If he had stayed home, you'd be an American!" I told him gleefully. "Hm. I suppose," he said after a moment's thought), an inheritance from a seventeenth-century patroonship larger than Dutchess County before New Amsterdam had become New York. He had run off with the seventeen-year-old daughter of an English diplomat and eventually settled in Australia, where he made a fortune in wool. His son resettled in England

11

and became a Royal Navy officer. Gus had been born there, in Ottery St. Mary. He had been best man at my wedding, and had known Georgia when he was five, and again when she was ten and he had been returned from China at twelve. Like all kids, Gus took his own history for granted, and was far more impressed with my grandfather, who had once owned John L. Sullivan.

Now, out of the neglected, unforgotten pages of the mind's manuscript of childhood, my oldest friend, Gus Van Duren, was walking across the Salmon Bar with his hand extended, crowing with delight.

"Neil, you've come back."

"I don't believe it. I was going to call you in London next week. Gus, you look great. How've you been?"

He waved to the barman, who drew two pints and then brought them over.

"William, this Yank here is my best friend, Neil Kelly. Neil, Will Hayhurst."

"Mr. Kelly, welcome again."

"I like your inn, Mr. Hayhurst."

"Everyone calls me Will or William. No need for a mister."

Gus leaned back and looked at me. "I've never been better in my life. Absolutely on top of it. You on your sabbatical? Can't wait to show you my new office. No, not London, not anymore. Down here."

His answers and question cut across another one I was asking, and we both stopped and laughed and raised a mug.

"Confusion to our enemies!"

"Let us now praise famous grandfathers!"

"Tin shoo po yaw!"

"I thought you'd never leave your practice in London."

He brushed it away. "Gave it up. The return of the native, six months ago. My own firm. Marvelous opportunities for some intelligent building here. You'll see. I can say without fear of contradiction that I am the best architect in town. The only one. Dinner with a client just done. Pounds galore, raking it in like mad."

He gestured expansively. "But much more important

12

news than that. What's different?" He posed to me. I looked, but except that he was stouter and had a thinner crop of ashy blond hair, he was the same. "Come on, what's the last imaginable thing for old Gus?"

"You're getting married."

"Got it in one. Almost. I swear to you, I am already married. And—"

"Hey, congratulations. How come I never heard, state secret?" I was pleased for the obvious happiness he was expressing, and mildly amazed. There are some men whose friends finally give up ever expecting them to get married. They are not homosexuals or neurotics, just bachelors.

"I suppose the honest answer is that we've been so absorbed in a world of our own creation that we chose to ignore everyone else and all the conventions. Wait until you meet her. Susanna Fox Van Duren. Neil, you won't believe how lucky I feel. I go around in a state of grace, and it's all Sue. She's . . ."

He was at a loss for words, like all lovers. The mind was mapping new territory for experience to ground the future in.

"Is she from here?"

"No, no. We met in London. Huge family, pots of it from mining. Father's a viscount. Accent like a Lawrence character when he's on about anything."

We drank and laughed. We were falling into the rhythms of a private language we had invented more than forty years ago out of the quick Americanisms of my family and the oblique and understated English idiom of his.

"But there's more, man, there's more." He raised his mug and cocked his head jauntily.

Only one thing makes a man look as if he's ready to take on the world. "You're going to be a father."

"I *am* a father. Got it? Ever hear of such an astonishing, altogether grand thing in your life? I. Am. A. Father. Four days ago. A boy. Richard Arthur Van Duren." We drank another toast.

"He looks exactly like Sue, except maybe for my ears. I wanted to call him Neil, I really did, but Sue would have

13

none of it. They've got a gaga uncle named Neil in the family, and she wasn't risking it."

"Gus, I think that's great. You really are on top of it, aren't you?"

He was nearly beside himself with pleasure, and promptly launched into a detailed account of how Richard Arthur had navigated himself into the world, an absolutely unique process thought by all nonparents to be simply the same everywhere. He finally brought himself up short, embarrassed by his own naiveté and emotion.

"I suppose you've heard about this sort of thing before. Been a father yourself, all that. You think I'm a nit, don't you?"

"I had forgotten how thrilling it is. Besides, I only had girls. You have it over me there."

"Listen, Neil, that's true for me, the very special quality of his being a boy. God, I sound like a pig. I promise you, if Richard had been a girl, she would have been loved and rejoiced in and wondered at, too. But I'm the same age you are, see, and Sue is forty. We didn't know if she could have a child at all, and then, instant baby. We were like kids discovering Christmas. And we both know there might not be another. Am I a pig for some additional satisfaction in having a son?"

"Yes, but what the hell." We both whooped and laughed and punched each other in the arm like schoolboys.

"We should have half a champagne." He looked toward the barman expectantly.

"Whoa. Not on top of my jet lag and the scrumpy and that pint. I'm out of shape for serious drinking."

"Neil, will you do me the greatest favor in the world and be Richard's godfather? If you don't it will probably have to be Sue's brother, Anthony, who's a bit of a horse's ass and who will moan and bitch about flying down from Scotland for it and God knows what else."

"I'd be honored, Gus. When?"

While I answered him, my mind was already making an instinctive dark connection with the title. I had been godfather to a girl in America who had been brutally mur-

14

dered. A goose walked over a grave somewhere, and I lifted my glass again to mask a tremor.

"As soon as we can arrange it with the vicar. Why wait? You're here. We're sort of Anglicans now, you know. Most people since Vatican Two can't tell the difference anyway, except possibly that we keep more of the Latin than the Romans do. Is that all right with you?"

"You forget that I was married in St. Mary's. Georgia and I started our own ecumenical movement a long time ago. Really, it will be an honor."

"I've not even asked you about your plans. Are you here for a few months? A few weeks? A year? Didn't I hear from someone that you were involved in some frightful murder at your college? One of your students? It must have been ghastly. Where are you going to be living?"

His questions tumbled out in an apologetic tide, mixed with grumbled curses against himself for being a self-centered boor.

I explained what had happened to my carefully pre-arranged housing for the spring. I knew he'd understand without elaboration what a bad time late April is for trying to make housing arrangements in the southwest of England. The tourist season is in second gear, and Americans, Germans, Japanese, and even British tourists are thick on the ground, grabbing up every bit of decent housing.

Gus was jubilant. "I can help you. I can, really. Do you insist on a cottage of your own, or would you settle for a self-serve flat in a good old Georgian building?"

I made beggars-can't-be-choosers shrugs of resignation. "I'd settle for whatever I can get now if it permits me some quiet for getting my research and writing organized. I'm so far behind on this book that I'm losing sight of it over the horizon."

He pulled out an envelope and a pencil and quickly sketched the layout of a one-bedroom apartment with a living room behind a huge bay window. "This is just a sketch. Look here. Second floor of a vast Georgian place I bought on spec and rehabilitated last year. At first I thought that Sue and I might live in the ground-floor flat—it's right on

15

the sea—but she would have none of it once we knew the baby was coming. I'm renting the seven flats for about two hundred pounds furnished, on average. I thought I had a tenant from Germany, an architect I met briefly in London, for the top flat there—what you call the third floor, actually—but his firm changed his plans for him. I've an advert in a couple of places right now, but I'll just shred the replies and it's yours for as long as you want. Quiet neighbors. All retired, as far as I can tell."

"If you'll let me pay the regular rent."

"Balls. Not you. Godfather bribe. I'll fiddle it on my taxes somehow, never fear. I have a marvelous, devious accountant."

I winced asking it, but I had to know where it was. "I really have to be near stores and so on. I don't plan to try driving the English roads again, and I'll need a daily shopping trip."

"Perfect. Little town, village, really. Stores and the rest right at your door. It's just five miles down from here, right on the coast. Literally. Raleighston. Sir Walter Raleigh was supposed to have gone for a bathe there or something." He pointed to his sketch. "Your bay window looks down over the beach onto Lyme Bay southward."

I was overwhelmed by my good luck and by the sudden collapse of my inner dread about going around to real estate agents tomorrow. I accepted in a haze of relief and pleasurable expectation. The luxury of a seaside flat in a decently restored mansion seemed too much even to have hoped for.

"Marvelous. Then it's settled." Gus patted his ample middle with pleasure and took out a curved pipe. "Mind?" I brushed away his polite question. He stuffed the thing and lit it and drew on it with all the holy attention serious pipe-smokers reserve for those rites.

Then he began to tell me about his new house, one, apparently, of which the strong-minded Sue approved whole-heartedly. In the process he bragged some more about her virtues and about the really extraordinary gifts already displayed by their offspring.

16

"He holds his head up, now you can't tell me that isn't precocious. And he smiles, Neil. I'm not talking about gas, the child smiles at us."

It was good to let him play his new role and boast his new happiness, and it was a long, happy evening for both of us by the time we finished.

I walked him out to his car and we talked about my daughters. I had to admit that I was badly out of touch with their mysteriously complicated lives in California, except for the occasional letter. I could almost hear his inner resolve that *that* would never happen with him and his son.

He finally said it. "I hope it doesn't sound completely fatuous to say that I fully intend to be very close to Richard as long as I live. It seems to me that a father and a son—" He laughed ruefully. "Shut me up."

"Shut up, then. If he doesn't seem as keen on that as you are, don't be too surprised. My own girls are eccentrics. I admit that I haven't a clue what they think they are making of their lives. But they seem reasonably happy. In their eccentric ways."

"They say it skips a generation."

"That would explain both my stodginess and their kookiness, so perhaps they are right."

"The Commander would probably think them the most normal of children."

"Yes, I think we both know whom to thank for any weirdos in my family, don't we?"

He laughed and recited. " 'Jeremy Jonathan Joseph Jones.' "

" 'The weather is far too dry.' "

" 'So I reckon I'll have to stir my bones, and try the effect of concussive tones—' "

" 'Upon a lazy sky.' "

We had recited it just this way, line and line alternately, at an American Embassy party in Peking in 1936. I had found the poem in an old copy of *Life* magazine, and although everybody else seemed embarrassed, our performance tickled the Commander for a week. He kept asking us to recite it again every time he'd see us together.

17

" 'So Jeremy Jonathan Joseph went/ away to the nearest town,' "

" 'And there his money was quickly spent/ for queer contraptions all intent/ to make the rain come down.' "

" 'There were cannon, and mortars, and lots of shells—' "

" 'And dynamite by the ton/ With a gas balloon and a chime of bells,' "

" 'And various other mystic spells/ to overcloud the sun . . .' "

Neither of us missed a line through the eight verses. Jeremy Jonathan made it rain, all right, but drowned half the county before the Weather Bureau stopped the deluge by predicting rain.

Gus was weak with laughter. We were reeling like two drunks, pounding each other's back.

"Oh, my God, where did that come from? That old doggerel. God rest his soul." He saluted the sky. "The Commander, your remarkable father the rainmaker, should have been an Englishman, you know. He was a genius, I suppose, but even you will admit he was one of the great eccentrics of his time."

I watched the sky a moment, letting my night vision sort out the clouds. The Commander had taught me that, and it was habit now. At a quick squint I'd have said that more stratus was blowing in at about five thousand feet from the west.

"He was that. John Stuart Mill, you know, said that the incidence of genius in any population will be roughly proportional to both eccentricity and moral character."

We left it at that. We both knew that my poor father, who had lived most of his life bewildered by the inability of people around him to understand his ideas, and who'd died bust, a failure in several fields of endeavor, had possessed a fair share of all three traits.

Gus couldn't pick me up until Sunday, so I made plans to stay at the Fisherman two extra days; he promised to be there bright and early Sunday morning to move me into my new digs.

18

*　*　*

Perhaps my father should have been born an Englishman, although even the British officials were likely to look askance at him in what we called Peking then, what now is called Beijing and somehow will never sound right even though it is closer to the Chinese.

If they could have seen him at home, with me and my mother, they would have looked even more askance. At least his appearance in his Navy uniform at state functions gave him the general outward appearance of an ordinary, somewhat superannuated American navy commander. Even then there was something—the askew tilt of his cap, or the rather shocking slouch he had even when standing at attention, which was not only unmilitary, but slightly against the laws of physics. He seemed always just about to fall over or fall apart. I had realized the first time I was drunk at a college party that I *felt* the way the Commander always looked. His commanding officer on his first ship had said to him in exasperation, "Kelly, you're just a few degrees off true north." I imagine Pa smiled his lopsided smile; he certainly did when he told us that story later on. It was a smile that charmed women and children, but put most men off from entrusting him with anything very serious. That smile, as much as any other single thing, probably kept him from ever being promoted past commander. He had been asked more than once why he hadn't been a chaplain. Or even a civilian.

I knew that the answer to the first had been my mother. As I lay in bed I thought of the two of them together, Pa always talking, explaining, Ma always listening with her head to one side.

He had met her during his second year at Annapolis, just when he had decided to transfer to Georgetown to become a Jesuit priest. He wanted to be a Jesuit, he said, because they had always been interested in meteorology. The answer to the second—why he stayed in the navy at all, against his own nature and increasingly against the will of the navy—was just as simple. He believed that he could teach the navy something it needed to know, but didn't know it needed to

19

know. Pa had a theory. He had it the way saints have a vocation—saints and other crackpots.

The navy is full of young officers with theories; they get them when they first go to sea and stand long watches at night. The sense of being alone and in on some important secret with God and nature is strong, and a man of the right temperament can be in trouble. He is likely to do the most dangerous thing there is in such cases, which is shut down his logical thinking equipment and begin to meditate. Any desert mystic or Zen monk will tell you that can lead to a lot of sudden, powerful, convincing, and absurd conclusions.

The Commander's theory was that whoever knew most about the weather would win the next war. To him that precept was what the idea of sea power had been to Admiral Mahan, air power to Billy Mitchell. Pa had got it from Vilhjalmur Stefansson, the great Icelander who went to divinity school and then studied anthropology, and then led a dozen Arctic expeditions. Stefansson was spiritual brother to all weather crackpots, and perhaps a special twin to the Commander. They quoted each other.

Pa sent me to a camp in Vermont when I was fourteen because Stefansson was a regular campfire storyteller there. I would watch that broad, sad face with the hooded eyes and the deep lines down around the mouth, a face like an old Indian chief under a shock of loose white hair, and listen to his Eskimo yarns and his predictions that the next war would be won by the side that had the best way of predicting the weather. He was as much of an influence as Pa in getting me to become a meteorologist in the navy when the war came a few years later. One night Stefansson said, ". . . as my old friend Commander Kelly predicted ten years ago," and I snapped awake from a half doze realizing that he was talking about Pa.

"What's your father?"
"Attaché."
"Permanent staff?"
"Rather. Mum says he's being punished."
"Whaddid he do?"

20

"Mum says he offended the Second Lord."

"Who's he? I thought you were Catholics, same as us."

"We are Catholics. The Second Lord of the Admiralty. He's an admiral in the R.N. My dad disagreed with him about submarines. In a very vulgar and obscene way, while under the influence of wine in his club, my cousin said."

"We're Catholics and my dad disagrees with admirals about everything and you were almost born in America. We might as well be brothers, for Pete's sake. Do you like it here?"

"It's not so awfully bad for chaps. Do you think so?"

"I think it's great. I'm learning to speak Chinese. *Tin shoo po yaw.*"

"I say. What?"

"In case you sneeze. I said, 'God bless you.' "

"Oh, that's good. Do say it again."

"*Tin shoo po yaw.*"

He bowed. "Thank you velly much."

We both broke up laughing at our own humor. The pidgin blessing was to become our password. I think two kindred seven-year-old lost souls were recognizing each other or creating each other out of lonely desperation. It was 1932.

Our chatter had started after Mass one Sunday, when we spotted each other, shoes shined and hair slicked, sidling out of church in the crowd, both staying as far as possible from uniformed fathers and hatted and gloved mothers.

"Hi, I'm Neil Kelly. My father's that one," pointing behind my hand to the Commander.

"Mine's"—indicating in the same shielded gesture a tall, thin English captain walking with his hands behind his back, bent and listening attentively to a voluble Chinese gentleman in a silk suit. "I'm Austin Van Duren."

"What do they call you?"

"Austin Van Duren." He seemed puzzled by the question.

"I mean Austin or Van or what?"

"Oh, Gus, actually."

It was my turn to look puzzled. I picked up a piece of gravel and threw it at a gate.

"You see," he explained gravely, "Austin is really a form of Augustine, so my family started calling me Baby Gus."

He spit skillfully to indicate what he thought of that, which started another round of laughing and pushing and spitting for distance.

21

"What school?"

"Here in Peking? Or at home?"

"Here, of course, Gus-Gus old spitter." It was my first try at his English accent, and it brought down the house.

"The British Infant School here, I'm afraid, Neil old fart." More hilarity. "Mum says at home I'd be for St. George's, Ascot."

"I'd murder them if they sent me to any American Infant School. Holy cripes." I hoped he was enjoying my profanity as much as I did his. "I go to Staff School, you know, just for embassy families. Mrs. Empson, Lieutenant Empson's wife, is the teacher. She knows some neato books she reads to us on the floor."

"Really? We read on the floor, too."

We were both dazzled by this incredible coincidence, and dodged and pushed our way the ten blocks back to the Legation Quarter exchanging information, insults, and swear words, and staggering under the impact of our own wit.

The Legation Quarter was our neighborhood. We weren't really supposed to leave it without grownups, but who cared about that? Gus lived in a big house on the grounds of a palace the emperor K'ang Hsi had built and which the British rented for their embassy, all two hundred rooms, surrounded by gardens bigger than the whole American compound. The palace was up on Canal Street, next to the Russians and across from the Japanese. We lived down on the Ch'ien Men corner, across from the old railroad station in a junky old fake colonial building the Americans had built for themselves. Gus envied me the railroad station and the noisy, lively market. I envied him his fairy-tale palace.

Our parents met while they were looking for us outside the cathedral, but we didn't know that until we each got punished later.

3

I PLACED A call to my home in Massachusetts just before noon the next day. I wanted to catch my house-sitter, a student named Bradley Oakes, before he left for the morning. I knew he'd be up early anyway, probably doing pushups on the bedroom floor. Bradley was for the most part a student of physical fitness. His friends called him Oaf, were glad he was on every Old Hampton sports team, and helped him pass his exams and write his term papers.

I wanted to tell him what my new address would be. Otherwise my mail, including my leave stipend from the bursar's office, was going to be bouncing around between home and Ottery St. Mary.

"Yo."

"Bradley, this is Professor Kelly."

"Hey. Did you hear about the robbery already?"

Calmly. "I haven't heard anything, Bradley. I've called to tell you I'm changing my address here in England. Do you have something to write with?"

"Gee, I don't know."

I could picture him, lying there on the rug next to the bed, looking wildly around on the floor for a pencil.

"I guess I'll have to go down to the library, Professor Kelly. I was doing sit-ups up here in the bedroom. I was just at two hundred. Hang on." The phone smashed down on the bedside table. "Sorry." He had picked it up to apologize, at least. He was back on the line in thirty seconds. "Shoot."

I gave him the new address in Raleighston, which Gus had written out for me.

"Got it. You want me to tell the college office, too?"

Oh, very good, Oaf. "Yes, please do that."

"It's funny. Someone called about fifteen minutes ago — I was just starting my sit-ups — asking for your address over there. Whoever they are, they got the old one. Oh, I gave the old one to the cops, too, after the robbery, so I'll tell them, too, okay?"

I was beginning to believe that there had been a robbery at my house.

"Who robbed whom, Bradley?"

"Two guys. Last evening. Burglary, I guess is the right term. That's what the cops said. You. They burgled or robbed or whatever you. About eight o'clock. In a seventy-nine Ford Econoline van. I was coming back from practice, you know, just jogging easy to hold my sweat until I could take a shower here. The fieldhouse showers are getting fixed again. It's a drag. So these two guys are just loading a trunk or something into the van in your driveway. So I go up to them and I say, 'Hey, what's going on?' One of them says, 'Take it easy,' so I say 'Take it easy my ass. I'm taking care of this house, so show me in writing you're supposed to take anything out or just walk it back in.' I can see the back door on the side there is open, so I figure these guys are thieves. Can you still hear me?"

"Oh, I can hear you fine, Bradley. I don't like what I'm hearing, but tell it all."

"Well, so the big guy gives me a shove and gets into the van. I can see he's got a hunting knife in a sheath on the seat. Then the little guy must've hit me with a wrench or something from behind, because I thought my skull broke open, and the next thing I knew they were split city and I was laying in your driveway with a big cut on my head. Not much blood though, about four stitches, I had worse than that twice in hockey last season. So I came in the house and called the cops."

"What did the police do?"

"They just asked a lot of questions, and I told them what I told you, and they checked around to see if anything was missing. We had those inventory lists you put in every room for me. But your silverware and books and everything were all okay. They said it looked as if all they took was the trunk out of the attic. There were three up there, weren't there?

24

'Cause there's just two now. You never gave me any inventory for the attic."

I tried to picture the attic of my house. Mostly old boxes of books and papers, and three old trunks ranged along under the eaves: a navy footlocker I hadn't looked into in years, full of outgrown uniforms and souvenirs; one gigantic old steamer trunk, locked and empty, which had been there when I bought the house; and my old black tin traveling trunk I had brought back from China, with my collection of traveling stickers on it.

"Which one did they take?"

"It had a gold dragon painted on the top. They left the big empty one and the Navy one."

My old trunk from China. Why that? "I suppose they might have been starting to clean everything out, top to bottom, and your coming along frightened them off."

I could almost hear him brightening up on the other end of the line. "You think so? I didn't leave it unlocked, you know. They jimmied the back door. It's in the police report. But, hey, maybe I shouldn't have left that note to Allen on the door saying I'd be back about nine, huh?"

Now I thought perhaps I could hear him wincing.

"It's usually a pretty bad idea to leave notes on your door saying you're away, Bradley, even in Oldhampton." He grunted contritely. "Listen, what's done is done. Call the locksmith over by the laudromat and have them put a new lock on immediately. You're sure that nothing in my library was disturbed?"

"I keep it locked. It was still locked when they left, and the cops looked in there, too, and nothing was disturbed. I mostly live in the kitchen, the john, and the bedroom, so it was easy to check. I figure it saves housekeeping, you know?"

"Well, thank you for taking care of it, Bradley, and I really am sorry you got knocked on the head. Are you okay?"

"Ah, that's nothing. Allen says they couldn't have hit me in a better place. No concussion or anything. I'm not plan-

25

ning to sue you or anything." He laughed good-naturedly at his own humor.

I told him I'd call again in a week or so to find out any further news, and hung up. It was the first time I had felt grateful for Bradley's thick head.

That evening, not yet fully prepared to accept any account given by Oaf, I placed a call to the police chief of Oldhampton, an old acquaintance of mine.

Cheif Scalli's familiar rasp and profanity greeted me and made no delay in getting down to business. At overseas rates I could be grateful for once that he had no small talk except for some insulting banter he used for punctuation.

"Professor. Even when you're away, you give me a headache. Me and that Oaf."

"Good afternoon, Chief. I understand my house was broken into."

"Yeah. You got burgled all right. You talk to that kid you got living there they call Oaf?"

"Yes. He told me that two men took a trunk from my house about eight in the evening and hit him on the head when he tried to stop them."

"Right. And broke the lock on your back door. He's okay. Doctor said he's got a head like a block of concrete."

"What else can you tell me, Chief? Was it a couple of fraternity boys pulling a prank? I mean, an old trunk."

"Yeah, well, you tell me. Was there anything valuable in it?"

"Not to my knowledge. I haven't even looked in it for more than twenty years. Schoolboy junk."

"Whaddya remember being in it exactly, Professor? To the best of your recollection?"

"Some old souvenirs of China. The trunk was probably more valuable than the contents, just because it had a nicely drawn dragon on the lid. But even that would have made it worth only forty or fifty dollars. My father gave it to me when I was ten. Really, nothing but toys, old clothes—beyond that I couldn't say. I grew up there, you know, in China, so I kept some of the odd things."

"No kidding."

26

"I can assure you there were no jade Buddhas or uncut emeralds or Sung Dynasty paintings rolled in spyglasses in it. I was twelve when I left China. What does a twelve-year-old have?"

"Yeah. Well, they were after something. Pros, I'm pretty sure, from the job on the lock. Maybe dumb pros, there's a lot of them around."

"I suppose it's gone for good."

"Like hell. Hey, don't I take care of my people, Professor? We got your trunk right here in the station. A little worse for wear, you know, but it's sitting right here in my goddam office. Andy Dombrowski found it in a ditch down his onion farm, called me."

"Well, thank you. That's wonderful."

"Yeah. That Oaf kid says it's the one he saw those two comedians putting in the van. Not too many trunks with gold dragons and a lot of stickers on them from Peking and Hong Kong and like that."

"Was anything left in it?"

"Looks like everything was. A lot of kid's junk, like you said. A model ship, some model airplanes, a wooden box with army and navy badges in it, a whole shitload of those quilted jackets and pants and cloth shoes like the ones the kids at the college wear now. And ten Mexican silver dollars, wrapped in a first communion suit, looks like."

My tenth birthday present.

"What on earth was the point?"

"I was hoping you'd tell me, Professor. Looks to me like they thought it would have something else in it, and when they went through it and didn't find it, they just dumped it in the nearest ditch."

"I'm grateful you recovered it for me. Will you hold it there until I get back?"

"Like hell. We'll look it over, fingerprints and like that, then I'll get Sweeny to drive it over to your house and give it to your guy. I got no room here. My wife says she'd like it for our front hall, I don't take it back she might burgle the station." He gargled at his joke. The talk was getting too small now to pay these rates for it.

"Fine. Thanks again, Chief."

"Yeah. Well, take care of yourself, Professor. Don't get mixed up with any more spies and so on."

"I don't intend to, Chief."

I had forgotten the odd fact that Mexican dollars were the standard currency in Peking then. God knows why. I had squirreled my birthday money away in my dragon trunk to be the nest egg for the eventual purchase of my own ham radio, an enthusiasm that lasted about a month. Gus's father, Captain Van Duren, had tried to interest both of us in studying radio, and for a short period while we learned Morse code and practiced tickling the transmission key, it seemed enchanting. Both of us lost interest quickly.

Gus's parents, I know now, never did wholly approve of me or my family. Like so many other mildly disapproving acquaintances, though, Captain Van Duren had been charmed and amused by the Commander. My mother rather fawned on the Van Durens; she was an Anglophile and worshipped pedigrees of all sorts.

Captain Van Duren had apparently been a child prodigy in languages, and had gone up from St. George's to Winchester and on to Merton College, Oxford, as what they airily called a "postmaster." My father explained to me that it was probably some kind of work-study job, but it proved to be British understatement for a *portionis magister*, a foundation scholar of the college, rather a lofty academic honor.

The captain had joined the RN in some kind of running war with his own father, who, like all adventurers, wanted settled sons. He had successfully dissembled his skills in the Sinitic languages until the fatal drunken duel of words with the Second Lord, who had instructed the RN to find for the communications officer Van Duren forthwith remoter employment. They had discovered his Chinese fluency and shipped him to Peking to direct naval communications at the embassy. He was at least glad that I had got Gus to take Chinese seriously, and made his wife also learn elementary Chinese. For a while he directed the Instructional Section of the Secretariat, the branch of the embassy responsible for indoctrinating fledgling consuls into the linguistic and cultural mysteries of their new foreign hosts. Gus and I found ourselves the only scholars under thirty, sitting in narrow, high-backed upholstered chairs beside the instructor's

28

desk, studying Chinese ideograms and reciting our pat phrases in singsong along with the third consuls, attachés, undersecretaries, and sweating junior officers in their stiff uniforms. For all the world like little princes, which I suppose, in a way, we were.

Because we played with our age mates in the Legation Quarter every day, who included, along with a stubby German girl named Frieda and twin Russian boys named Pitirim and Nicholas, two elegant Japanese children, Seiji and Tokiko, who both already spoke Chinese, we gained a great advantage over our old classmates. They, typical European adults, would leave class and studiously avoid uttering a syllable of undemanded Chinese or encountering a Chinese merchant face to face. They would speak to their servants in pidgin. We would take each day's phrases—"How much is that?" "I am an Englishman," "Good morning, you are looking fit"—and run screaming them at Seiji and Toki, who would cheerfully insult our pronunciation and scream them back at us until we were all racing up and down Canal Street and through the magic gardens of the British palace chanting and improving our vocabularies. We called ourselves Our Gang.

Gus had something of his father's gift; I had to work much harder at it. I asked him one day if he was going to study Chinese stuff when he grew up.

"Not bloody likely. I'm going to be a jockey."

"Wow. I'm going to be a radio announcer. Pa says more people listen to Lowell Thomas than anyone in the world." I was trying really hard then, at eight, to make my voice more resonant, but no one seemed to notice.

"I suppose you can always read the news in Chinese if no one back in the States will hire you on radio."

"Oh yeah, well, you're going to be a pretty fat jockey."

That was the sum of our serious discussion of vocations.

Gus became an architect, of course, although he took the same detour through the navy that a lot of us had to take in 1942. He had then started studying art history, but decided he'd be an artist and went to Slade for a while before he went to Edinburgh and became a qualified architect.

4

GUS INTRODUCED ME to Sue and to his new son at lunch on Sunday. Before that, true to his word, he showed up at the inn at nine to move me to my new digs in Raleighston. He gave me a tour of the area on the way.

The village sits between outcroppings of low red cliff at the edge of the English Channel, with a stand of pine behind the town itself. I was to discover quickly that the locals didn't agree on whether they lived in a town or a village; it seemed to depend on which division of the "Britain in Bloom" competition they wanted to be listed in. The population hovered around one thousand. No one mentioned the dog population, which was at least that.

Raleighston had, in its heyday, been a fishing village. While the pilchard, the once ubiquitous cousin of the herring, had made its annual appearance, the locals had flourished. A combination of fishermen's skill, greed, and perhaps a change in the flow of the Gulf Stream had caused the pilchard population to drop to almost zero, and the unemployed boatmen hereabouts had turned with a will to smuggling and wrecking. More than one local fortune was traceable to profits from those two thriving enterprises. A few of them had built mansions above the low cliffs. Then, in Edwardian times the town had attracted leisured gentry looking for seaside places to erect their terraces, and a modest start was made on tourism. It was then that a few decent pubs and inns had sprung up, the best of them, according to Gus, being the Raleigh's Cask, where we stopped for a breakfast before doing any moving in.

The sign above the entrance, with its painting of a ruffed and bearded head in a golden helmet, made it clear that the original of "Cask" had been "Casque": Raleigh's helmet.

The owner, Andrew Sharpe, was behind the bar tallying his stock. He dried a hand on his apron and shook mine firmly.

"Any friend of Mr. Van Duren's."

"You'll probably be seeing a lot of him, Andrew. Perhaps you'll be forced to chuck him out a time or two. Professor Kelly is moving into one of my flats."

"We'll take care of him, sir, don't worry at all about it." The patron put down his work good-naturedly and rubbed his hands together. "I have a piece of bacon you'll enjoy if I put a few eggs with it, I think. And Mrs. Sharpe's Irish soda bread is just baked."

"Not too early, is it, Andrew?"

"We do a bed and breakfast, and so we are ready to provide a bit of food any time of the morning. It's no trouble at all."

As I was to discover, the people of Devon are easily the kindest, most courteous people in the English-speaking world. We ate kingly. I knew I had found my local.

"If the apartment is half as good as the pub, Gus, I'll take it. Otherwise I'm moving in here."

The building itself was on Fore Street, bordering the sea at the eastern limit of the town. Its back was to the street, so that the residents could have full advantage of the breathtaking view out over Lyme Bay toward France and the south.

Gus pointed with his pipe as we stood in the small formal garden between the house and the stony beach. "Channel Islands, Jersey, Guernsey, so on, about eighty miles due south. Boat goes there from Weymouth, just up the coast."

We went in the side entrance and up the six half-flights of stairs to my new apartment, each of us hiking one of my bags. Gus handed me the keys. We went in, and I was hooked at first sight.

The living room was to our left, and did indeed have a wide bay window overlooking the water. From this height the white-painted room was dazzling in a flood of sunlight, and the soft blues in which the simple modern furniture was

31

upholstered took me back instantly to a place Georgia and I had once rented on Provincetown Harbor.

I couldn't get enough of the view from the window, and stared out over the blue sea hungrily. "It's exactly like that room in the final scenes of *The French Lieutenant's Woman*."

Gus grinned appreciatively. "I rather think so too. She lived just a few miles east of here, after all." He grabbed my arm and rushed me back to see my kitchen and bedroom, pointing out the merits of the place. The place had probably once been servants' sleeping quarters when a single family and their help had occupied the space now accommodating seven apartments. It was snug, new, and unmarred.

We went back into the living room and I saw the pair of bottles on the tiny mantlepiece for the first time. I stopped in the middle of a word. If it was the first time I saw them here, it was far from the first time I had seen them. Those two Kyoto pottery bottles had stood on the mantle in our house in Peking forty years before.

Gus watched me with unfeigned delight as I sat down on the sofa with the two bottles in my hands.

"You sly dog, where did these come from? They're the ones from our house in Peking, aren't they?"

They were far from being treasures, although they were moderately expensive. Pa had bought them for my mother for their tenth anniversary, and they were probably her favorite things she had in China. The bodies were covered with crackled beige glaze, and the blue-green enamels, bamboos and plum blossoms, were thick and opaque, eighteenth-century style. The mouths were rimmed with gold, and, just as I remembered, the neck of each one was closed with a small wax plug my mother had put there. They stood no more than ten inches high, a perfectly matched little pair.

"You had probably forgotten it, but when my family shipped me back to England after the Japs came in thirty-seven, long before they evacuated you, your father persuaded mine, God knows how, to take a trunkload of his

32

effects along with me. Do you remember that flat tin trunk with the golden dragon painted on the lid?"

I did now. There were two of them. Pa had given me one and used one himself.

"Do you have it?"

He laughed and banged his pipe out into the fireplace. "I didn't even realize I had until moving forced me to drag out stuff I hadn't touched in years. Then I met you and thought perhaps I'd surprise you with these. Don't they take one back to Peking, just sitting there?"

I set the bottles reverently on the mantlepiece. "Is the trunk in the car?"

"Uh uh, at my house. I drove down here already once this morning to put these here. What larks, eh?"

"If I look amazed and grateful, I am." I walked over to the window and the spectacular view again. I had two questions to ask him, and I didn't want either to sound paranoid or just barmy.

"Gus, this is absolutely perfect. Bless Mrs. Will Banky and her brat for expropriating my cottage."

"I couldn't be more pleased if I were getting actual rent for it." He shook his head and puffed on his pipe, pleased at my pleasure.

"Just remind me, Gus: what else was in that trunk?"

"Ninety percent of it your father's famous scientific notebooks. A couple of boxes of photos. Another piece of porcelain or pottery of some kind, Chinese. That's about it. These two were obviously the prize. The Commander must have been afraid that if the Japs came round taking an inventory, they might look unkindly on anyone holding what was probably Japanese loot in the first instance."

"I suppose." I traced the bamboo branch on one of the bottles with the tip of my finger, dissembling my next question with a joke. "Not much burglary around here, I hope."

"God. I doubt if there's any measurable crime rate in Raleigh. Few yobs on motorbikes zooming around trying to look nasty, or the odd drunk pissing on a wall. Unlike dear old London, I might add. You sound like Sue. She wants me to install a burglar alarm on the new house. I gather her father's been at her about it. He lives in a damn fort up there in Scotland, really. Damned if I'll do it to protect a lot of Fox family heirlooms. Dog, perhaps, hm?"

"Surely every English boy should grow up with a dog."

"I don't blame you for laughing. Englishmen and their damned dogs. You'll soon find out in Raleigh. These retired admirals around here seem to go in for small, hairy beasties at a great rate. I like a good-sized dog, don't you?"

"I'm not a dog man, I'm afraid, Gus."

"Not a Doberman or an attack mastiff or that sort of thing, but a decent-sized dog Richard can climb on and rely on to give him a bit of protection, hm?"

I glanced at him quickly. From his tone, he was serious about protecting Richard.

He added a hasty footnote. "Not to worry, of course. I'm not exactly head of NATO or an oil tycoon. Italian fellow put the bee in Sue's bonnet about all the kidnappings there, and she has been at me ever since. I can't really convince her that no one is going to snatch our son and heir for a million pounds ransom."

We locked up the apartment, leaving my bags unpacked, and set off for Ottery to meet Sue and Richard for lunch.

The Commander had believed passionately that the Japanese would eventually take China away from the shaky coalition of European powers and Chinese warlords who claimed to rule it. He believed it when it was a very unpopular point of view, but it was probably his sanest idea, and the most ridiculed. Especially by Gus's father.

They would sit in our cramped living room playing chess and arguing half the night.

"Go ahead and laugh. Japan, my Limey friend, is in the same situation England once was. Worse. A crowded island nation with the will to be an industrial giant. All they lack is the raw materials."

"Japan, Commander, is a paper tiger, as our Chinese friends would say."

"They lack the raw materials but they're sitting in a position rather like my queen there, to move out in any direction and take them."

"Really? With the British in Hong Kong and Singapore? With

34

the Americans in the Philippines and Guam? And the Dutch in the East Indies? The French in Indo-China? Protect your bishop, Commander, or your queen isn't going to be worth a damn to you."

"Coal and iron here, rubber and oil to the south. Everything they need. Tanaka explained it all back in nineteen twenty-seven. They'll take it all."

"Oh, really, Kelly. Using wooden boats and paper aeroplanes? The Japs are the wogs of the Far East. Not worth a damn as soldiers or sailors, and too timid to drive out their own aborigines up in Hokkaido."

"They are doing some remarkable things with weather forecasting, you know."

"Aha, now we have it." He moved his knight pawn warily. "No wonder you admire the little bastards."

"What is the British budget for weather services, Van?"

"Good Lord, how would I know? Negligible, I dare say. The English have always rather waited for the weather than gone out to look for it, you know."

That set off a new round of debate and chess moves.

Pa would never get off that subject if he could be allowed to get on it. "The great and free goddam republic of which I am representative here at the moment spends slightly less than two cents per capita for its entire weather service, know that?"

"I doubt if anyone in the world but you knows that."

"That's beginning at Point Barrow, Alaska, and going down to Hawaii, and from the Canal to Maine. Two goddam cents, Van."

"Perhaps that's what it's worth, Commander. All that business of flying balloons and drawing pictures of storms at sea."

"Bunch of lunkheads. Two cents per capita, per lunkhead."

"A penny too much, probably. Check."

"Like hell. If they would increase it by exactly one penny per capita and give that increase to me, with a free hand to establish an experimental weather station somewhere—Guam, Manila; hell, right here on the roof of this building—I'd show them something worth ten battleships. Fifty battleships."

"I say, how did you do that? My jolly old castle is looking rather threatened, isn't it? Doomed, actually."

"And can your jolly old king and queen be far behind?" Pa asked slyly.

"You rascal. Were you preparing that all along, or was it just a bit of inspired luck?"

5

GUS'S HOUSE WAS actually not in Ottery St. Mary, but in a little Ottery side village of Raleigh's Gill, just south. A gill is a brook in this part of the world.

When we pulled into the yard of his new house, we sat in the car for a few minutes and he pointed out the features of the original structure still discernible and the remodeling and expansions. It was a low, slate-roofed, sprawling affair of dark stone and wood that seemed to have been built in random sections starting about 1700.

"There she stands, Neil. Actually, I never imagined, even a few years ago, that I'd yearn for a country squire's estate, a place of me own, ye know, awa' fro' the city lights."

" 'The irresistible, universal, automatic tendency to find sweet pleasure somewhere, which pervades all life, from the meanest to the highest, had at length mastered . . . ' Gus." I smiled at him sweetly. "Hardy must have been writing not far from this place in Wessex when he wrote that about Tess."

He stuffed his pipe into his jacket. "Ugh. Nasty book. Dark and full of murder. Made a lovely film, though, even if none of the landscapes were actually Wessex."

I changed the subject back to what he obviously wanted it to be, his house. "You've left a lot of the original. At least to my ignorant eye it appears that way."

"Hell of a job at first," Gus moaned. "I was sure I had bitched it after we took off that north end to put the ell along there and bring the whole side a little more into proportion. Then it occurred to me that all I had to do was . . . C'mon, I'll show you." We slid out of the car and tramped around to the north side. Gus pointed and explained in simplified terms as he went, proud as a peacock. Last year's brown bracken was still in the yard with the new green

36

growth, and we had to push our way past a thick cascade of ivy overhanging the corner of the wall. A brown creeper hitched himself part way down the trunk of a cherry laurel to have a look at us, then flew off.

"Whole property's a mess," Gus said, seeing me survey it. It looked about an acre in extent, running downhill slightly to a small brook that he said joined the Otter somewhere a quarter mile down the road. "Bit boggy there toward the gill. Damned boggy, to tell the truth. I'll build a play yard, sandbox, that sort of stuff up this end, away from the muck. That's my June project, if I ever get all my May projects done." He hesitated before saying, "I'm thinking of giving it a name. Does that strike you as insufferable, too bloody English for words and all that?"

"Yes, if you're going to call it something like Stately Acre. Not if it's a reasonable name."

He grimaced. "Richard's Gill, actually."

I wasn't about to step into what must be an important matter between him and Sue. I evaded the need for a direct reply the way academics have done since Plato: I quoted literature. " 'May her bridegroom bring her to a house, where all's accustomed, ceremonious. . . . How but in custom and in ceremony are innocence and beauty born? Ceremony's a name for the rich horn, and custom for the spreading laurel tree.' "

"Hmm. Shakespere?"

"Sounds like. Yeats. A poem for his first infant, a daughter."

He paused, one hand on the open door. "Uh, Neil, it's Richard. Never Dick or Dickie or any of that lark, hm?"

I smiled and winked at him. "Gotcha."

Sue was nursing Richard when we entered. They were in a plain black Boston rocker by the south window of the dining room, bathed in sunlight. I could not have met either of them under conditions better suited for appreciating my friend's new happiness.

The mother made no attempt to rise, simply made a gesture that took in herself and infant and lifted her face for Gus to kiss.

"I'm so happy to meet you, Neil."

"And I you and your son. You two look like a Renoir painting."

Gus was simultaneously embarrassed that he had boasted in the car that lunch would be ready, solicitous that we not disturb the baby, and vain of his beautiful family. I let him endure it. Husbands must be allowed to learn from experience, no amount of theory will ever cover it.

Sue was truly a long-legged beauty, a bit bony, but in the way now fashionable, and with an immensely wide, perfect smile that lit up her face. The baby, from what one could see of him burrowing in, was a sturdy, reddish article with great staring dark blue eyes.

The parents exchanged small talk about how many minutes he was feeding and how many ounces he was gaining now compared with his birth weight and losses in the first two days.

Gus could not quite control his eagerness to hold his heir up for my inspection. "Is he almost through eating?"

She cocked her head and growled at him in the broad Yorkshire accent that must have been their private language, "If tha want t'boy, he'll be nobbut a minute."

Gus ticked the corner of his mouth and looked loving and helpless. A new father is a personality astray in a new field of force; a new mother has simply lost her own margin and assimilated herself with the new field.

Lunch was already prepared, as it turned out, and only needed bringing in from the kitchen. It was obvious that a good architect had designed the efficient spaces of that room. Gus showed me where he had ripped out a mud room and a second porch and a pantry to create the space around a central butcher-block island under a canopy of copper pans and exotic utensils. We carried mugs and plates into the dining room.

We ate cold roast beef sandwiches, on thick sliced bread, and tomatoes, and drank the local cider, which they warned me had the kick of a good ale, but was lively and tangy on the tongue.

Sue was an easy, perceptive hostess, and kept one eye on sleepy Richard on her shoulder while still managing to make me feel that my visit was the most interesting event of her day. She pumped me enthusiastically for details of Gus's boyhood. He had told her little about Our Gang in Peking, and she laughed and clapped the baby on the back, hearing my stories and his sputtered protests.

"Really, Neil, Gus told me none of this."

"Because it was not nearly so colorful. Anyway, Neil, you have the facts wrong. Wasn't it the market on the corner of Water Gate Road where what's his name, the little Dutch kid, Piet, who never could figure out what was going on, ran into the old bitch being carried in the palanquin and knocked her out into the road?"

"No, no, remember? It was Pitirim."

We went on for an hour before Gus said, "Enough, enough about bloody China. Let me tell you about my lovely wife." He raised his glass.

She colored and rolled up her eyes silently.

"Let us drink to the newest author in this land of literary genius. Sue has a book coming out."

I drank to that. "Congratulations. Fiction? Nonfiction? Poetry? What?"

She held her fingertips a half inch apart. "A little teeny paperback for a series about great historical figures. Mine is John Wesley. I did a thesis on him once, so while I was carrying Richard and couldn't exactly race about after Austin here, I dug out my old notes and wrote a sort of popular Everyman's Guide to John Wesley."

"Isn't that marvelous?" Gus beamed.

Sue put her right hand on her bosom and trilled in a Beatles' falsetto, "I wanna be a paperback write-ah!"

It was an easy, lovely way to meet the family of my best friend. There was something as happy as holiness among them, and for a short time I was being let in.

"She'd never tell you herself, but they want her to do another one. Libby Grandisson, her editor, thinks she's a natural storyteller."

"He'd never admit to you that what they won't let me do is the one I want most to write: Oliver Goldsmith. 'Rural mirth and manners,' y'know."

The sated child emitted a contented burp.

I said, "A photograph of Richard right now would do nicely to illustrate 'his best companions and his best riches.'"

Sue sighed. "Why did I ever marry an architect when there are men out there in the world who have read Goldsmith. To Gus: 'innocence and health and ignorance of wealth,' darling."

"Hmph." Gus touched his son's cheek with a forefinger. "Well, he'll lose two of those soon enough, won't he? May he hang onto his health, at least."

I knew it was time to make my exit and let them have themselves to themselves for a while. Since Gus was my ride back to Raleighston, I said I hoped they'd let me wander around the neighborhood and explore the bank of the river a bit before leaving.

"Fine," Gus said, "as long as you don't get lost. I'll be ready to drive you after I kiss my wife properly and use the loo."

Sue, who had put the baby in his cradle and was clearing dishes, stopped to remind herself of something. "Oh, Gus? Someone called and said that he'd call back this evening. From London. Francis Lee. Do you know a Francis Lee?"

Gus obviously made the same association I did, because he asked his wife, "Li? Chinese?"

"Heavens no. British. Veddy plummy and BBC."

Gus exchanged glances with me and shrugged. "Maybe it's a new client."

As I walked down along the gill toward the river, trying to stay clear of the red mud and not succeeding very well, I wondered if it might not be someone rather different.

The only Chinese who eventually became part of Our Gang was Francis Li.

His family, which seemed to comprise some twenty or thirty, an equal number of servants, and squads of children, took up

40

residence in the Wagon-Lits. It was the hotel in the Legation Quarter, squeezed in between the German and Russian embassies on the corner of the Water Gate, kitty-corner from Gus's on Canal Street. It had been built for European visitors to their legations, but in times of political turmoil we all became accustomed to wealthy Chinese clans arriving by the wagonload with their servants and valuables, including their opium pipes and concubines, to shelter until the storm outside had passed and they knew with certainty which warlord now controlled their old neighborhood.

Francis had spotted us spying on his family's frantic influx, the men shouting and gesturing, the black braids of the hotel maids flying behind them as they raced back and forth with armloads of boxes. He was short even for a Chinese boy, probably a year or two older than I was, but at first we thought he was about five.

Gus greeted him rudely in fluent Chinese, telling him to go home, little boy, or the running dogs of Europe would eat him up.

Francis couldn't have been more delighted. Black eyes twinkling, and giggling at every step, he raced across Canal Street and faced us, rattling breathlessly away and pointing toward the Ch'ien Men. His face was scrunched up with excitement, and his beaky nose made him look like a fat little owl.

Gus was the first to understand him, and he whooped with delight relaying the good news to the rest of us.

One army, led by the so-called Christian Marshal, Feng, had rebelled against the army of Wu, their allies, and was about to capture the city. The city soldiers were running for the hills and the rickshaw boys were fleeing for cover so they wouldn't be pressed into service pulling army supplies outside the city for its defense.

"They are building a gate of triumph for Feng down at Ch'ien Men," the dancing, excited boy told us. "I am Francis Li. We are Christians, and when Feng comes, my father will be even greater then he is now. But now we must wait here, you see, in case Feng does not come at all." He laughed his high-pitched, excited giggle.

It was typical. The early-warning systems of the street people and servants had provided them with better intelligence than the entire European assembly of legations. There hadn't even been a call-up of reserves from the barracks to protect the embassies.

41

Our Gang huddled and decided that if we told our fathers, they would only whisk us off the street behind embassy walls—if they believed us at all. It was clear to all of us that the only thing to do was to get lickety-split down to the Ch'ien Men and see the grand entry of Marshal Feng through the triumphal arch they were building.

Led, astonishingly, by Francis, who could run like a deer, we beat it down to the market. There was indeed a twenty-foot-high gateway of four thick poles and a crisscross of wooden strips being festooned with black and magenta paper roses going up near the train station entrance. Apparently they did not know if the Christian Marshal was coming by train or on horseback.

A handful of disgusted soldiers were whacking camels loaded with military gear through the gate outward, and some rickshaw boys who had not escaped the general draft were hauling officers and their equipment in the same direction. Francis told us the soldiers were paid a flat fee of two and a half Mexican dollars per battle. The rickshaw pullers got nothing.

Then, in an explosion of curses, fleeing, tipping rickshaws, and screaming sergeants, the Christian Marshal made his appearance out of the dust. He was in a motor car driven one-handed by a gesturing, cursing officer, and he and his staff were making a panic retreat away from a battle they had lost interest in, taking the shortcut through the city to escape.

The workmen winding the ropes of pink paper roses over the framework of the triumphal arch kept right on with their decorating. Someone was going to come through that gate a winner, even if it wasn't Feng.

We cheered and cursed the fleeing general staff in seven languages, Francis Li leading the chorus, even though this probably meant that his family was not going to get richer soon.

Twenty minutes after Feng had raced through the arch, his pursuer, the victorious Manchurian General Chang, trotted his horses through the same gate, completed now, bowing and smiling. His brown-skinned, stony-faced troops were strung out behind him for half a mile.

I saw his eyes widen with amazement for a moment as he spotted Our Gang, a clot of white and brown faces and waving hands, and heard a small, shrill voice call out in perfect Manchu, "Manchu women are only good for whores! Manchu men aren't good for anything!"

Francis had won his place in Our Gang with that sally. We

raced away shrieking into the American legation, just across the street, where we found the secretary on the phone sweating and swearing and trying to find out what was going on. He seemed astonished when nine-year-old Neil Kelly explained it to him, backed up by a polyglot chorus of agreement. He kept saying, "Are you sure? Are you sure?"

6

ON MONDAY I fought off the temptation to stay snugged in bed beneath the enveloping warmth of the quilt and listen to the sea. It was pounding louder, faster, than it had been when it put me to sleep. That meant a south wind, directly in off the Channel, and that promised a fair morning.

I looked out over the wide slice of green Lyme Bay. I had learned, among other bits of local usage, that the scallop-shell indentation in which my house was set was known as Tricia Bay, and that the Judas tree in the garden was called Tricia's Penny tree, perhaps a half-remembered story connected with some child who had once lived in the mansion.

The sun was well up, and there were lines of whitecaps everywhere, the sea sparkling and racing to heave its green tons on Tricia's beach.

An elderly, dignified dog was walking his man and woman along the water's edge. Raleigh had played there as a boy. I had seen in the Tate the Millais painting of young Walter Raleigh and his half brother, Humphrey Gilbert, which the town boasted had been painted down there.

Perhaps Donne had walked here, too. No record, but negative evidence can't be weighed. It had been edging into my mind that I might try writing a poem in the manner of Donne, a sea poem. It would be no lugubrious and nostalgic "Dover Beach," for sure. More like: *When did we ever bathe except naked in this sea . . .*

My mind was wandering. I knew it was time to walk to the cafe for my breakfast. The hot sausage rolls would be ready, their pastry as light as croissants. The hilarious local newspaper, which was rapidly becoming my favorite entertainment, would be in the store where Kathleen would fold it for me and sell it to me with a queenly smile.

44

I knew that I had better start a workday then, or I'd lose another day in mooching around. Getting to know the neighborhood was grand fun, but the book was dying of malnutrition. When scholars start composing bad imitations of real poets instead of getting off their swanboat and onto business, they are invariably goofing off.

Elizabeth, in her inevitable blue smock, knew me well enough to start pouring coffee for me as soon as I came through the door of the cafe.

"I have some nice hot scones and fresh Devon clotted cream for you, Professor. Eh?"

I sighed at the demise of another good resolution. "Just two, Elizabeth. All right, with cream. And the usual sausage roll."

"A bit of jam wouldn't hurt anything, would it?" Elizabeth had joined that mysteriously cooperative, worldwide conspiracy of women who see me and want to fatten me up. Another dead resolution.

"Jam, then."

I ate in kingly isolation. The cafe wouldn't really be busy for another half hour. The *Southwest News* was its usual comic self. Headlines over a three-village war about a right-of-way on a footpath. Lost corgi found amid tears and laughter. Man fined heavily for firing a beer mug through a mirror in Exmouth, despite his plea in defense that he had eighteen pints taken since noon and was not in full control. Local heats of Miss East Devon — a headline I decided not to pursue. Incomprehensible sports page. Apparently Australia had scored 194 runs in the first inning against England. Take out the pitcher, was the only advice I had for England. Ottery St. Mary cottage vandalized. Something suddenly familiar, in a small item on an inside page, under exclusive photos of the Queen's 1956 visit to lucky, loyal Devon.

Brown Cottage, a rental property on the Gillan House estates in Ottery St. Mary, was the scene of a disgraceful smash and grab Saturday night.

The tenants, a woman and child from Newcastle, Mrs. Will

45

Banky, a widow, and her son Richard, were away at the time in Sidmouth for the Meat Bingo.

When they returned at about eleven, the cottage door was broken, and inside they found a litter of tipped and torn belongings. Although they found nothing actually stolen, a set of Mrs. Banky's matched toiletries were smashed, and Richard Banky's stamp collection books were torn and thrown into a brook nearby. A sad and vicious piece of malicious mischief. "I think it's an outrage," the distraught widow said to our man.

Mrs. Laureen Gilbert, the caretaker of the Gillan Estates, said it was the second time this season that suspicious activities have occurred.

The police are investigating, and ask that anyone who saw anything suspicious or any strangers in the area recently call Exmouth 4651.

I knew better than to think it was a coincidence, but I also knew better than to think it was not. Was there the slightest point in calling the police to tell them what I suspected, on the basis of no evidence at all: that perhaps the vandals in the Banky's cottage and the burglars who had taken a trunk from my house three thousand miles away were somehow connected? To ask the question was to answer it; there was no point.

By four that afternoon, just at about the time I had given up trying to pump some life into a paragraph on the Nineteenth Elegy, the police called on me.

The young constable I had seen rocking on his heels outside the post office each morning about nine was standing in my doorway. He asked me politely if I was Professor Neil Kelly, and could he stop in for a bit of a chat if it wasn't too much trouble, just a question or two.

La Gilbert had put them on my trail. Detective Constable Howe explained with a pained seriousness more than half embarrassment that the caretaker at the Gillan Estates in Ottery St. Mary had suggested that I might know something

46

about certain events which had taken place there the previous Saturday night.

"I don't know if you're aware, sir, but there was a bit of vandalism there, a holiday cottage torn up a bit."

"Yes, Constable, I read about it."

"You being a professional man, sir, it isn't that we think you were off in Ottery on Saturday night on a tear, but Mrs. Gilbert, she's the caretaker—"

"We met."

"So she says. She suggested that when you were there last"—he consulted a notebook—"Thursday, you were in a somewhat excited state. Seems that you had booked this Brown Cottage and failed to appear within a week, so she let it to the Bankys? She didn't seem sure if you were a professor of literature, I'm sorry to say. She said that you had never heard of Samuel Coleridge, the poet from Ottery, and she found that a bit suspicious and so on."

He raised both eyebrows and scratched his ear with the brim of his helmet.

"I suppose it would be no trouble for you to let me see your academic identification?" He blushed.

I produced my faculty ID from the college and he copied information from it laboriously into his notebook and handed it back to me.

"Thank you, sir. Very good." He seemed relieved and at some loss what to say next. He put his pencil and notebook away, then took them out again. "Can you give me any suggestion, Professor Kelly, whether you saw any suspicious persons about when you were there? In the area or hitchhiking or the like?" He scratched his ear again. "We talked with the lad picked you up and took you to the inn."

The Devon and Cornwall constabulary were no one's fools.

"Between you and me, sir, I think some yobs from Sidmouth were out having a bit of dirty fun. Leather jacket lads, you know. Teds, we call them over here."

"We have them too, Constable. We call them all sorts of things." He smiled and raised both eyebrows again. "I will tell you one funny thing, though."

47

"A funny thing? What's that, sir?"

"My own home, back in the States, was burglarized just this past week. I spoke to my caretaker about it by phone just on Friday."

"Is that so, sir? Amazing coincidence."

"It would have been, wouldn't it, if I had been living in Brown Cottage as planned? As it is, perhaps not quite so amazing."

"I see what you mean." He jotted a note and put his equipment away again and fiddled with the strap on his helmet. "Well, thank you, Professor. I think we won't be bothering you again. Are you staying here for a few weeks' holiday, just in case there should be any reason to chat again?"

"Come back anytime. I'll be here for six months. I'm on leave from my college," gesturing hopelessly at the litter of papers and books on my work table by the window, "and I have a book to write."

"I hope the lovely view isn't too much of a distraction." Constable Howe finally found the proper balance for his helmet back on his head and adjusted the chin strap with the tips of his fingers. "What kind of a book is it, sir, if I may ask."

"Well, it's a sort of a mystery, Constable."

"Not a murder mystery, I hope. Scares me, it does, the number of people who read crime stories and get ideas from them."

I looked properly horrified and sympathetic at the suggestion I wrote such low stuff.

"More of a literary mystery. I'm trying to figure out why a poet became a priest."

"Ah, a literary mystery. There's no end to human nature, is there, Professor?"

And that, as it was to turn out, was precisely the definition of the problem. Of human nature there is neither height of holiness nor width of stupidity nor depth of wickedness nor end of any kind.

On Wednesday the sun came up yellow through a thickening overcast and I knew it was going to be no day for a walk along the cliffs. With the historic city of Exeter less than fifteen miles upriver, and with a direct bus leaving just after eight, I decided to scratch an old itch and go to see The Exeter Book. Anglo-Saxon poetry is not my field, but teachers are the most eager tourists of all, and I had seen many photographs of the incredibly beautiful calligraphy and I wanted to look at the original.

Exeter is a city the Germans once described as a jewel they had bombed into total destruction. But long before that, others had tried destroying it and failed. The Romans had wrecked the first Exeter and rebuilt it as *Isca Dumnoniorum*, and the Normans were to take their turn and end by building on the Saxon and Roman ruins they made. The brutes who boast of their powers of destruction come and go; Exeter stays and grows, still partially walled, full of the remains of those earlier conquerors.

The Cathedral Church of St. Peter looks exactly as I had imagined a medieval cathedral should look when I was a boy. Square, turreted, symmetrical Decorative Gothic, a storybook church with golden weathervanes like flying pennants. That the parish church in Ottery St. Mary where Georgia and I had been married was a miniature copy of it only reinforced my fondness for its unique architecture.

The Cathedral library is in the Bishop's Palace behind it, in modest rooms on the second floor. There, directly inside the door, The Exeter Book rests under glass. The script looks almost Arabic in its long, severe beauty, the pen strokes like knife cuts, the paper as white as when it was made.

I looked at the double open page for a long time. The Anglo-Saxon of my student days failed me completely, and I had to settle for a silent admiration of the work of design each word is. The librarian, a young, bearded graduate student from the university, to all appearances, glanced at me incuriously and returned to his hunt-and-peck typing, dismissing me as another wandering American tourist with no idea what he was seeing except that it was Very Old.

I moved over and read half a page of the tiny Latin script

of the Domesday Book, the census report of William the Conqueror, which sits beside The Exeter in its own sealed case, then went over to ask the typist if I might buy a facsimile of a page. I knew that my old friend Macready, who taught Early English at Old Hampton, would be pleased to have one.

"You can only be admitted to the regular collection if you have some scholarly identification, sir. Are you interested in studying the facsimile, or do you just want me to Xerox a page for you?"

I produced my academic identification, which he studied intensely.

"You're Neil Kelly." It was an announcement rather than an inquiry.

I agreed that I was.

"But you're the Henry Vernon man."

I knew I was in safe hands. A seventeenth-century man. "Yes, well, I have written about him. Frankly, I have always doubted whether anyone but me had ever read it, though."

"Marvelous little book. You simply made hash of old Jaccobi and his zany ideas about Donne writing those poems. I'm so happy to meet you." He stood and shook my hand enthusiastically. Then he insisted I sign the guest book, which I did.

"I'm Thomas Wall," he explained as I was still writing. "I'm a graduate student at the University of Exeter."

Since he was watching me inscribe my signature as if I were about to pass a miracle, I thought to add under the "Comments" column, in modest Latin, a comment that scholarship, like a great library, is supported by its Walls.

He blushed beet red. "I say, I say," was apparently all that he was able to think of to say.

Nobody but a few specialists ever cared much, but about ten years previously a wild man named Jaccobi from Amherst had "discovered" a previously unknown Donne poem, and had traced it to Donne's late, religious period. Which would have made it very remarkable indeed, since it was a fierce erotic poem of the sort the poet had stopped writing at that stage in his career. Jaccobi had subsequently produced from the same faked treasure trove four other complete poems and a fragment, all spurious Donne. I had refused to join the chorus of praise and hallelujah, which reached even the pages of respectable journals, leave *Time* aside. Eventually, by means that it would bore a layman to death even to hear about, I had tracked down the man whose work the minor poems were, a nineteenth-century hack and forger named Henry Vernon, an American from Pawtucket, Rhode Island.

"We had to read the whole episode in Metaphysical Poets last year. Professor Bush said your book was a model of historical inquiry."

I liked Professor Bush, whoever he was, as much as I did young Thomas Wall.

We settled on which page of The Exeter they would photocopy for me as soon as the woman with the key to the Xerox machine came in.

Wall's obvious pleasure in our meeting and the care with which he talked about Donne made me sure of one thing: he was one of those students marked for the profession. After thirty years I could tell the merely eager ones from the future scholars intuitively. The eager ones sometimes actually knew more, and did better on exams. But in the end the true student who would become the honest scholar and teacher, and make his mark, was distinguished by his sheer love of what he was talking about rather than of himself. It is as real and as unmistakable as a young man's monologues about his first romantic love.

On an impulse I invited Wall to join me for lunch, partly because he would be able to tell me a great deal more about the contents of that libary, and partly just because he was such a decent, enthusiastic young man.

We lunched at The White Hart, a fourteenth-century inn, under hand-hacked black wood beams, and drank a bitter called Davey's Wallop. He told me that he wanted to write a book about Duns Scotus, the medieval genius whose originality had got his philosophy dismissed as the work of "a dunce" and whose few loyal students were called dunces. It was a good hour. He was a terrifically bright, modest

51

young man with relatively few whacky ideas for a graduate student, and the whole thing made me feel more back in touch with my work than anything else since I had been in England. I collected my Xeroxed page and went back to Raleighston with renewed energy.

7

A GODSON REQUIRES, in addition to the obligatory rattle or curved spoon, three gifts: a boat, a ball, and a kite. Even my poor neglected book's mute complaints couldn't be allowed to stand in the way of that. I had worked two days straight, accomplished ten pages I wasn't entirely ashamed of, and I voted myself a holiday.

Since they were necessities, I saw no point in delaying their purchase, even if the recipient would not be ready to play with them for a year or two.

Thank God for the trains and buses of England. They will take you anywhere. On time.

To Plymouth, for example. More ships have set out from Plymouth, I suppose, than from anywhere else in England. Drake and Raleigh sailed from there, so did the *Mayflower* folks. And Francis Chichester, and many millions more, great and small, in between. It is a place where the making of boats for boys is done properly, with loving attention to their shape, their size, and their color. On Saturday, at noon, I was walking down the great Parade in Plymouth.

The toll of German air raids here had been colossal, some seventy thousand buildings destroyed. But from old St. Andrew's Cross to Derry's the Parade was open, clean, and as attractive as a modern shopping center can be.

I stood on the Citadel Walk, along the uneven rim of the Hoe, and gazed out over the famous sound. A small sailing vessel was tacking toward Drake's Island. Then, wandering through the maze of fifteenth-century streets and alleys that make the Barbican, I found, above the Barbican Steps on Castle Street, first an interesting new restaurant that I noted, then, above it, in a corner of the old castle yard, the model shop of Bartholomew Barling. The old toymaker, nine-tenths of whose stock consisted of marine miniatures

53

and ship models, was someone I had visited a long time ago, and I had wondered if even his shop, let alone the man, would still be found.

The son looked like the dead father, and the shop was now his. He was just as attentive to my explanation of what I wanted as his father would have been, and he sold me a gorgeous double-ended red dory, twenty inches of scarlet wood with a single thwart across its four-inch beam. Too small to take the weight of a brave three-year-old who might try to launch himself out into a pond, but just about right to accept a small stuffed bear in a sailor suit as a passenger.

At the tiny Barbican Steps, I lunched on the best barbecued beef I had ever eaten, and then walked with my bulky package under my arm along the quay, taking in the harbor sights, taking in the sun. I knew exactly what my bones wanted on a slow, small errand like this. I had come to England to recreate my own capacity for celebrating life, a minimum condition for celebrating Donne's life, and the bones know what is working.

I rested against the stone wall and watched a busload of Japanese take each other's pictures by the monument saying the *Mayflower* had left for America from this spot. I helped a woman glazed with fatigue put her five-year-old upright after he had toppled off a low wall he was trying to traverse on one leg.

I hugged my boat and my improving sense of myself, and basked in the weak sun.

After a boat, a ball. I knew that I had to go up to Cambridge anyway, to visit the Fitzwilliam and read a Donne manuscript there, one of the starting points for the section of my book I was about to write. I knew too, that just off Trumpington, before you reach the Fitz, in one of those twisty small alleys between where Christopher Marlowe had lived in his undergraduate days and where Richard Crashaw had sat with his tutor, there was a marvelous, cramped, crammed toyshop full to spilling with bright, mostly Scandinavian toys.

The woman in charge let me alone, wisely. I did those things one must do to shop properly. I squeezed, I juggled, I bounced, and I gravely compared the balls in a large wire bin. Large but not overwhelming is the key. Bright, but not garish. Tough. And rubber, not plastic.

She leaned across the counter appreciatively, seeing that I was near a decision. "I hope one will do," she said seriously.

One did. Large, for one-year-old hands, but manageable. Especially with the help of an obliging dog. Red, blue, and yellow; primary colors are best. Rubber. Swedish.

I left there happy and went to the Fitz, where seeing my old friend's notably clear, modern hand again in the holograph manuscript gave me a further improved sense that I was back in touch with my subject.

It had begun to rain when I left, but I had come prepared, raincoat over tweed jacket and my irreducibly shabby Irish walking hat. I protected my purchase—it was the flimsy bag that needed saving, not the ball—and walked leisurely up to the Turk's Head, a place I'd lunched often before when I could afford it. I had a slow lunch of chops and beer, then as noon arrived and the place filled up, I paid for my fare and walked back out into the rain.

Convalescence of the spirit requires approximately equal parts of sunshine and rain; the failure to realize that important rule is the mistake of those who go to places like Miami Beach to rest and find that they merely wither.

I sang quietly but exuberantly to myself, "I wanna be a paperback write-ah!" A good-looking woman passing me turned to stare. And some of that, too, perhaps. My mind paused a half note and reflected. It was the first infinitesimal awareness entering my consciousness that part of my reasons for shopping might be Sue and not only Richard. Or Gus. What Waugh somewhere calls a tiny batsqueak of sexuality. When our vital forces resurge, they return tangled.

Then it was time for a kite. Only the Chinese really know kites.

The first day of school in September for Chinese children was

55

traditionally called The Feast of the Ascension. It had nothing to do with the Christian feast of the same name; it was the day they all flew kites in the stiff east wind.

The ambassador thought it a charming idea to have the Legation Staff School begin its term in the Chinese way, chiefly because the Commander had planted the idea in his head at a cocktail party when the ambassador was quite drunk. As a result, the Commander and I would spend all of August making brilliant, glorious, gaudy box kites of rice paper and split bamboo. It didn't always coincide with the actual starting up of our classes, but as soon as the autumn winds were favorable, the teacher, Pa, and all the kids would trek out north of the city in the blue-covered Peking wagons drawn by tough little ponies and unlimber our creations.

Once the class had fourteen kites aloft at once, cylindrical lampshades, easy diamond shapes for the little kids, and, on one occasion, a twenty-five-disc dragon kite it took the two adults and me and Gus to control.

The government wouldn't give Pa a supply of balloons and hydrogen for upper-air observations, so, naturally, we made and flew kites. That was the real point of the whole exercise. The first-day-of-school lark was just a way of getting a budget for that, and it worked. The U.S. Weather Bureau had seven kite-flying stations across the United States then, and as soon as Pa read about it in a four-month-old copy of the Boston *Sunday American*, he started scheming to get his own kite works going. It almost ended as soon as it began when Pa applied to the secretary for funds to buy kite string.

"String? Kite string? I suppose that can go onto the school's budget without much harm."

"Thank you, sir. I'll order some, then."

As we were on the way out his office door: "Oh, Commander: er, how much string would that be, more or less?"

"I figure about four miles, Mr. Secretary."

The poor man looked shocked. We left and closed the door quietly while he wrote it in the ledger and thought about it.

The highest we ever got one of our box kites with instruments in it was 4,115 feet, measured in string. Among other things, people started saying about the Commander that he was going native, a rather serious charge in those ethnocentric days—a way of saying he was going nuts, really. But the Chinese nodded enthusiastic approval, although I noticed that somehow Francis Li was the only Chinese child allowed to join us on our Ascension Day kite fly.

If you take a Number 52 bus from Hyde Park Corner and get off at Portobello Road, you will be in one of the bargain hunter's heavens of London. Walk just a short distance down Portobello and watch the restaurant signs; you will eventually see one written in Chinese. No English translation. This lack of concession to tourist limitations had been what attracted me initially to enter the place years before, and ever since I had, it had remained one of my secret pleasures in the world's most pleasurable large city.

The sign said, if you could read it, *Ch'ien*, The Creative. Its logo was the first hexagram in the *I Ching*, which has that name. It is also called, for reasons that would take rather a long time to explain, The Flight of Headless Dragons. It reminded me of my home in Peking, across from the Ch'ien Gate.

The owner and his three workers, who were engaged in some sort of disagreement about a crate of goods, broke into four smiling, moving figures when I entered and stood for a moment, letting my eyes get used to the dark interior.

They were not the shopkeepers I had known, but I explained to a portly, shiny-faced, and completely bald fellow with hugely pop eyes what I required. I knew that my tones were rusty, but he looked impressed.

"You speak like a real northerner. Not Kwangtung, no, no. You are fortunate that you spoke to me. These boys speak that Cantonese gabble from the south. We appreciate the honor, you know, when a foreigner takes the time to learn our language."

He was one of the endlessly courteous, circumspect ones. I was no more going to be allowed simply to buy my kite and bow out than I was going to be allowed to speak English. This was going to have the pace and circumference of a tea ceremony.

First he had to call out and introduce each of his unworthy assistants. One son, two nephews. The scholastic honors of one were announced and admired, and the business acumen of another. The third, who was distinguished as the father of three sons at the age of twenty-one, was permitted to wait on the honored customer while the owner excused himself to complete an unfortunately already late business call. Would I understand? I would. Was I sure? I was.

After a half hour I had received a tour of the dining, drinking, wagering (Did I care to place a small bet on the outcome of any particular chance event I would care to name? No, I would not, thank you), delivery services, fireworks, and, finally, kite-making rooms. Several new cousins and four sisters took their bows. At last we were examining the hectic red, black, and gold designs on sheets of rice paper made for box kites. But suddenly a new voice, older than all the others as soon as it was recognizable, actually spoke my name.

"Neil Kelly. As I live and breathe. *Tin shoo po yaw.*"

I turned; it was Francis Li. Far stouter, grown gray, hair combed straight back in a harsh brush cut, but his pinched owl's face with its beaky nose and black eyes entirely familiar.

He embraced me like a short bear attacking his prey, his pudgy hands beating me on the back as the two of us exchanged exclamations of pleasure.

"What a marvelous surprise."

"And what a coincidence."

"Were you the Francis Li who called Gus last week?"

He giggled. "Yes, yes, that was I." He was bursting with glee. He took my arm and we ducked under the hanging kites in the shop to the rear room, where the owner silently bowed his way out of the cluttered office and left us alone.

"My cousin, you see," Francis said.

" . . . the last person I expected to see in London."

He held his hands apart as though measuring something large and laughed again. "I am very important number one boy in my government now, thank you velly much, you bet." He switched from his pidgin singsong to mellifluous English. "First you were in your embassy in my country, now the tables are reversed and I am here."

"Well, almost reversed. I wasn't a diplomat, I was a brat."

"As good as. You look so well, Neil. You are a famous scholar now, eh?"

"Gus has been talking. Not so famous. Just an ordinary run-of-the-mill professor of English literature, in a place called Oldhampton, Massachusetts."

"That is a name I will not try. It sounds like one should say God bless you again." He lit a cigarette and held it between his thumb and first finger, smoking in tiny puffs, squinting through the smoke.

"My name, by the bye, is no longer Francis, although I haven't the slightest objection to your using my old boyhood name. Now I am Li Chen." He shrugged and winked.

"You were in Peking through the revolution?"

He flipped his free hand back and forth. He had a dozen different cultural gestures; his whole body language was international. "Sometimes in, sometimes out in the country. For my health, y'know. I am a good Marxist now, do not fear. Some of us spent some uncomfortable days marching around the city with placards around our necks explaining the different sorts of vermin we were, but all that is past now." He threw up his hand theatrically. "Gone, poof, with the wind. What brings you to England?"

"Sabbatical study. I am trying to write a book about John Donne."

"There is so much I do not know, yet they call me a Minister of Culture. Please, in very few words, end my ignorance about this important person."

"A contemporary of Shakespere's. A poet. In his youth a famous lecher, in his old age a holy priest. Some think he betrayed his faith to get political preference and that his late piety was penance for the guilt he felt."

"What kind of poetry did he write?"

"Erotic, then religious."

"Good. I like him. Yin and yang.

"Perhaps yin and yang. But late, radical conversions are always suspect in some quarters."

"Touché. You are touching close to the quick, I think, in your clever way, Neil. Of course, St. Paul was older than I when he converted. Among others." He gasped and giggled and slapped his knee.

"We must all meet, eh?" He blew out a long train of smoke, made his eyes round, and laughed again. "You and Gus and I, the three musketeers of Our Gang. Oh, dear." He leaned forward conspiratorially. "Perhaps we had better not talk about Our Gang of three of any number, in case the word should get back to my superiors, who might wonder, eh? Who are these running dogs of capitalism Li Chen is getting ganged up with, eh?, they will ask." He screeched with laughter at his own melodrama. Francis had become slightly manic in his performing style.

Before we parted, with indefinite plans to meet for a reunion, he helped me pick out a simple diamond-shape kite for Gus's new son, yellow, with a showy butterfly painted on it. He was all atwitter to think of a present of his own to send.

He made the owner unwrap the kite sticks and rewrap them, sealing the ends better, lecturing the poor sweating man in hectic Chinese.

If Francis had been interested in his European and American age-mates, he had been fascinated by the Commander, who in turn thought Francis was a wonder.

Perhaps it all started when, ten minutes after being introduced to Francis, Pa asked him what he thought the chances were of the Kuomintang getting final control of China.

To a boy who was pampered by servants but generally ignored by adults, this adult, serious question from the American commander must have been an exotic, delicious experience. Within minutes the two of them were arguing in Chinese and English about Sun Yat Sen, the influence of the Russians on Chinese military training, the chances of a Communist takeover in Hunan, the price of flour, the Japan's ambitions in Asia.

Whether he believed Pa or not—I suspect now he was just exercising a natural gift for flattery and diplomatic chatter —Francis agreed with every one of Pa's theories by the time they were through talking.

"That's some kind of smart little nipper, that Francis," my father said at dinner. "Knows more than anyone in the embassy about the Soongs. I couldn't tell if he's related to them or what. Who's his father, anyway?"

"I don't know, Pa."

"Well, dammit, Neil, try to find out."

"Don't swear in front of the boy, Commander."

"Those Soongs run all the banking in China, is what I hear. And Francis thinks so, too. If the goddam Manchus aren't going to finance my hot-air pipeline along the Wall, maybe they will." He was off on one of his favorite pipe dreams. "We could make it snow on the damn Russians, you know, Mother, any time we pleased. Freeze their damn army in their tracks the other side of Sinkiang."

"Really, Commander."

When I did ask Francis offhand one day if he was related to the Soongs, he giggled and said, "Oh, yes. They are all my cousins. Many, many cousins."

Meanwhile my poor crackpot father kept working day and night, filling his notebooks with calculations of how much heat it would take to cause a rainstorm over the Gobi Desert. This at exactly the moment in history when a Dutchman named August Veraart was proving that the key to induced rainfall was seeding clouds with dry ice, not blowing steam heat up in the air.

An endless chain of events seemed always to be contradicting Pa's best expectations from his lonely experiments, but he never stopped expecting the next event to prove him right. That is surely the stigmata, the unmistakable sign of the elect, in a crackpot. I loved him, but he was a crazy saint in a church with just one member.

8

GUS PICKED ME up about one, and we drove back to his house in Raleigh's Gill. The godmother-designate, Sue's sister Edwina, pulled her Bentley into the yard about three seconds after we parked.

We gathered between the cars in the warm sunlight for introductions.

"Edwina, my oldest friend, Neil Kelly."

We exchanged polite expressions of delight and she said that she had heard a great deal about me from Sue.

"Will we all go in your car? Or take both cars, or what? What did Sue say?"

"Where's Don?"

I wondered who Don was as the family sorted out the arrangements. I suppose even the royal family get into this when they all have to go to the same place at once, unless an equerry or a footman in charge of protocol sorts them out and assigns them to cars, with no backtalk allowed.

"Oh, here he comes now. That wreck of his actually made it."

A battered MG, red with wire wheels, slung about three inches off the ground, a beat-up, undergraduate sort of car, sprayed gravel stopping inside the gate. We all migrated in a bunch over to the new arrival.

"Oh, Don,"—Edwina was ostentatiously shying away from letting the vehicle come into contact with her lilac coat—"why don't you get rid of this old thing?"

"Edwina, how marvelous to see you again. Gus. Nervous?" The newcomer, a beaming, fattish man in enormous glasses, his spare hair askew, put out his hand to me. "Donald Fox. You must be Neil, the godfather."

"Don's going to christen the baby, Neil," Gus interjected

as we shook hands. "The Vicar of St. Mary's didn't seem to mind a bit getting away this afternoon, did he?"

They all laughed at some inside family joke. So brother Don was actually Father Don.

"Whereas I considered it a joy to motor down from London for the occasion. Shall we all go inside and have a decent drink? I hope there's time. The clock in my car is a bit odd."

"Lovely."

"Good idea."

"How's the star, asleep?"

"Like an angel," Sue, who had greeted us all in the door, kissed him. "I'm going to let him, too, until the last minute. I want him in a good mood."

We entered the house in talking, gesturing pairs. The voices spread gently out into three or four linking conversations in the long living room. Gus went for drinks.

I stood with Sue and her sister while Sue explained that she didn't dare put the heirloom christening dress on Richard until just before departure.

"It's positively frail with age, you know. The lace is old Honiton. Queen Charlotte gave it to one of my grandmothers," she explained to me. "It was from her wedding dress."

"I thought you said this was a well-behaved child we were godparenting," Edwina said. "He doesn't jump around or do high kicks, does he?"

"My dear sister, like all babies, he wets his pants, and I'm afraid that the whole garment might crumple and come apart at the seams. He does it a lot, as a matter of fact. I do hope it's a healthy sign."

Edwina looked down at her lilac coat and sighed and said to me, "You hold him."

I was taken over to see the famous garment, laid out ironed and spread wide. It covered half the loveseat, with a hem of lace twenty inches deep, its length a man's height.

I found admiring things to say. My godson's mother's family, it was apparent, was well established in the peerage as well as being decidedly rich. The two don't always go together.

Gus brought in a tray of tulip glasses and Piper-Heidsieck and we toasted the sleeping child, the parents, the godparents, the sacrament, and the guest clergyman.

"Oh, Gus, Libby called. She is going to come for the service. Robert, too." She looked at him a bit out of the side of her eyes as she said it.

Gus pinched my arm. "Oh, oh, I'm afraid you're for it, Neil. Libby is an unattached woman."

I had a sinking feeling familiar from a hundred other social occasions. It is the instinct of the unmarried male telling him that the wife of a friend has picked out a widowed or divorced or single friend who would be just perfect for him.

Gus grinned and provided more information. "Libby Grandisson, Sue's editor. Somehow the subject of you being Richard's godfather came up in a phone conversation a half hour after you left us."

Sue was having none of his sly digs. "Libby is super, Neil, and Gus knows it. You're not going to be prejudiced against her just because she's a smashing, brilliant, articulate widow with a large income from her profession, are you? And, of course, she's a superb judge of books." She laughed. "And writers. Gus, she says Collins will let me do the Oliver Goldsmith. Actually."

That required another toast. She had cleverly switched her embarrassment away from matchmaking to her writing, a very classy Queen's pawn sacrifice of the sort that only great hostesses make instinctively.

She answered a further unspoken question, leaning closer to say something.

"Bobby's sort of her pet brother. He's quite retarded, and he adores Libby. She takes him everyplace and never explains or says a word, just sees to it that he has a nice time. There, how can you dislike a woman like that?"

"I shall try to be equal to this paragon." What else can you say?

"Sue, really, you are unscrupulous." Her husband steered

her across the room toward Don and Edwina, lecturing her in a stage whisper, but not lessening her apparent satisfaction with the arrangements she had made.

I took time to look around me. I had not been in this room on my first visit. It was a spacious L-shape, with a single grand rug, a cream and gold Bokhara approximately the size of my side yard at home.

A fine red oak chest on a stand, the drawer fronts and cornice crossbanded in rosewood, stood between the north windows, and an eight-foot mahogany breakfront bookcase covered the entire inside wall beyond the fireplace, its shelves containing a standing full set of Japanese *imari* plates and bowls, their blue, black, red, and gold underglaze glowing through the brocade design.

Gus took the canapé tray from the girl who had brought it in from the kitchen, temporary help for the party, apparently, and set it down on a George III mahogany bow front sideboard with narrow boxwood stringing lines.

Sue came back across the room and took a cigarette from the silver box on the sideboard and offered me one. "Gus wants me to quit. Ah, wise you. I've offered to if he will give up his filthy pipe."

She flipped the lid of the box and held it out with a grimace for my inspection. "This is about all that remains of my first marriage. Father had the announcement engraved, and I've never got round to having it scrolled or effaced or whatever one does. I suppose the grandchildren might like to have it as an example of mid-century bad taste."

I read the inscription hastily.

The Honourable Susanna Elizabeth Fox, younger daughter of Lord and Lady Fox of Gateley House, Evesham, Worcestershire, is to be married to Mr. Jeremy Morestone, 1st the Queen's Dragoon Guards, only son of Major J.C.S. Morestone, of Gibralter, and of Mrs. Morestone, of Wotton-under-Edge, Gloucestershire, at the parish church, Evesham, on June 6

"Jeremy was variously impotent, drunk, sadistic, and

cashiered. He drove his car into a tree in France ten years ago. Suicide, I imagine."

I tried to imagine the correct reply.

"So it's rather obvious, isn't it, why I gave up marriage as a bad job for twenty years, until Gus and I met in London."

"Gus swears you were engaged an hour after you met.. True, or poetic license?"

"Too true. A splendid, head-over-heels, old-fashioned, heart-in-my-mouth whirlwind courtship. I suppose we were unconsciously seeking each other, and the collision of purposes was rather earth-shaking for us both. Can you believe that?"

Oh, yes. "Gus is happier now than I've seen him since he was a boy racing his pony."

"Hah. Knock wood. I hope. Have you seen this rather special chair Gus gave me?" She showed me a Chippendale mahogany elbow chair near the doorway. Next to it on a period tea table was a small Enoch Wood bust of John Wesley. "It was Wesley's own chair. I'm thrilled to have it. And speaking of ponies . . ." she turned to speak to Gus across the room, where he stood with Don in front of the mantle looking at the instant pictures Don had been snapping since we started in on the toasts.

"Austin, you're going to love Father's christening gift for Richard. Gifts, actually. One for his house, if you please, when he's grown. The Stubbs painting of the harvest wagon that hangs in the London house, with those great fat horses, you know, the Wedgewood one? And, too predictable, Merry's foal by Trumpeter. He called from Scotland, all apologies and excuses for not being here, et cetera." She turned back to me. "Actually, my family hated the idea of my marrying Austin—you always call him Gus, don't you? I haven't got used to that yet—everyone did, I suppose, to be honest. That seemed to me the final confirmation of the rightness of the thing."

I could see, watching her in her own home, now much strength she had salvaged, nurtured, and stored up out of a life purposeless until she had met Gus. A happy woman in possession of her world has no nuances; her whole being is a distillation of joy.

Don brought over a batch of snaps for us to admire. The christening gown. A woman's shoulder and my profile, frowning. Gus and Sue, rather a pleasing composition, touching foreheads. A rather goofy shot of Gus proposing a toast. The home photos of the rich look very much like those of the poor. A kind of technological democracy has been imposed on us all by corporate godparents, Kodak and Polaroid.

Don Fox was an amiable, not terribly bright man, who seemed awfully fond of his sisters and quite puffed up about being an uncle. It was easy to get the impression that the Fox clan had about given up on having an heir in this generation, with Donald observing a rather aloof celibacy and Edwina having miscarried her only pregnancy before ending her short marriage to a Tory M.P. The patriarch of the clan, the remote viscount, was, to hear them chatter freely about it, almost imperceptibly thawing toward Gus since his contribution of Richard to the house, but still reserving any public approval.

The baby cried. The small party was instantly transformed into dashing preparations for the main event, the women assembling vestments for the child and the men huddling again over who would be going in which cars. Don and I both remembered that we had left gifts in the cars, and rushed out to retrieve them for presenting.

After I had left Francis on Thursday in London, my play presents for my godson in hand with the purchase of the kite, I shopped for something suitably impressive for a formal gift. A shop in the Piccadilly Arcade had yielded up, with the clerk showing every sign of reluctance, a George III silver and coral rattle (with whistle and comforter, as the breathless fellow had whispered to me importantly) by Samuel Pemberton. Even if Richard's parents weren't dazzled, I knew that the spirit of my mother would be wildly approving. Presented, it seemed an adequate success. The real presents, which were tossed in as an afterthought, still in their bags and store paper, amused everyone, as I was prepared they should.

Richard was produced in his candidate's outfit and wildly applauded, then photographed. He promptly did something that caused his mother to say, "Oh, God," and rush him back into the other room for changing again.

"That," Gus said gratefully, "gives me an opportunity to produce my own gift for the godfather." He took a book from the drawer of the sideboard and laid it across his arm like a headwaiter displaying a vintage wine for inspection of the label.

It was entitled *A Hidden Life*, and it was by the Oxford historian, Hugh Trevor-Roper. I took it gratefully. Anything by Trevor-Roper is worth owning, but exactly why I might find this of special interest still eluded me.

Gus was gleeful. "It's a biography of our old chum Sir Edmund Backhouse, W.C." He showed me the flap copy. "I rushed off and bought it after I met someone else we both knew in Peking. In London, this past week. You'll never guess in a million years."

"Ah, let me see. Francis Li."

"Bastard. Did he phone you? He sent that gorgeous silk wrap. Did you love his David Frost imitation, my God."

"We met. Really. He looks fatter and richer, and he says he's now officially Li Chen, some sort of under-minister of culture."

"Exactly. Apparently he's over here trying to recover the Chinese manuscripts he says Backhouse stole or some such, and gave to Oxford. There seems to be some doubt about whether Sir Edmund was putting them in the Bodleian Library for safekeeping or giving them over."

"Francis said we'd all get together soon. Did he fix a date with you?"

"Only one or two possible times. He'll call you, I think it was left at that."

Gus and I drank another glass of the champagne, which was already raising my voice, and chortled over the pages of Trevor-Roper's debunking study of the old fraud Backhouse, the so-called Hermit of Peking.

We had both, as children, seen the mysterious Englishman being drawn through the streets of Peking in his rickshaw, holding a handkerchief over his face, as he always did.

"Pee-Yew! There goes old Backhouse!" was our single and unfailing witticism. I had explained the American usage of the term to Gus the first time we had heard the name, and he was enchanted.

"I say, a backyard loo?"

Sir Edmund was actually one of the legendary figures of modern Chinese scholarship, and the collection at Oxford is accompanied by an inscription in marble expressing the gratitude of the University to him. But we did not know or care of such honors. Gus has even improved on my vulgarity with some of his own, and dubbed the old knight Sir Edmund Backhouse, W.C. We'd shout that out, too, sometimes, falling all over ourselves with lewd delight.

The burden of Trevor-Roper's study was the message that we had been closer to the truth than had Oxford. Sir Edmund had faked histories, forged manuscripts, translated classics he himself had written, and also, in his spare time, defrauded the British and American authorities of vast sums paid to him for negotiating deals he never made.

My father—he would, of course—had thought him an eccentric genius, and had made a dozen attempts to talk with Sir Edmund about Chinese science. He hoped to persuade him to use his influence with the Chinese government to finance a network of experimental weather stations across China. That and a dozen other schemes.

The baby reappeared and was freshly applauded. More pictures were snapped in the side yard. I rode to the church with the priest brother in his MG. The rest went in Edwina's Bentley.

The communal rite of Christian initiation, water, oil, and salt, was bestowed on Richard Arthur Van Duren by his uncle shortly after three P.M. on a May Sunday. The event, attended only by angels and by his real and surrogate families, took place precisely on the spot where, in 1772, the

Vicar of St. Mary's, Father Coleridge, had baptized his own thirteenth child, who was to grow to such literary eminence.

The identical words were spoken over Richard Arthur that had been spoken over Samuel Taylor. On the future poet's behalf two other godparents had pledged themselves to be concerned for his welfare as a Christian soul in pilgrimage, just as the Honourable Edwina Fox and I did for our sleeping, gently smiling child with the bubble of spit at the corner of his mouth. Undid the ribbon of his bonnet to bare his head for the water, loosed the neck of the family gown (how much use the Coleridges gave theirs!) so that a drop of chrism might touch his neck, and teased his cheek to encourage him to open his mouth to taste the bitterness of the salt of life.

I read the words of the Prophet Ezechiel, telling us that God would take away our hearts of stone, and the godmother said the words of John, that the world had been given its meaning before it was made, and that the meaning was love.

The glamour of evil was denied by us for him, and the grace of God was affirmed and brought down. The sacrament was complete; Richard Arthur was now our fellow Christian.

We stood together under the splendid fan vaulting in the Dorset Aisle by the ponderous Victorian marble font, being photographed, and made a symbolic community of love and protection for the child. It was, as the liturgy of the Mass says, altogether fitting and proper that we should do those things. And none of us could have added in the least to our hope for his well-being as we exchanged glances, touches, and kisses around him, completing the ceremony of his innocence.

Libby Grandisson and her brother Robert had arrived just as the ceremony was starting, tiptoeing in, all mimed apologies. If she was attentive to the American godfather, she was at least as attentive to her nice, rather helpless brother and everyone else. She was carrying a first edition Lewis Carroll in her bag, which she presented to the child as his first post-baptismal gift.

I studied her remarkable features and listened to her resonant, quiet laugh and realized I liked her very much immediately. She was full-lipped, with a short, straight nose and fine gray eyes. Somewhere I had seen features on a marble statue just like hers, both chiseled and soft. She had deep dimples when she smiled.

I distracted myself from her riveting good looks long enough to remember my offices as godfather and complete them. As the altar boy extinguished the last candle, I shook his hand. He palmed my five-pound note with the skill of a headwaiter.

We went out into the sun of the south churchyard for more pictures of the star under the iron sundial in the wall of the tower, each of us having a turn to hold him. They would be his last pictures. Within a week Richard Arthur Van Duren's life would be snuffed out, and along with his, the lives of two others who had stood laughing into the camera with Richard in their arms.

9

IT WAS CHESS, more than diplomatic duties or military strategies, that had brought our fathers together constantly. Gus and I were both disappointments to them in the matter of chess. Doting parents both, they had, at first, each encouraged our little hands to move the pieces for fun, then tried to whip up our enthusiasm, then tried everything else short of force to make chess partners of their sons.

Gus and I compared notes on their attempts to convert us to the idiotic pastime. We agreed to play worse and worse. It seemed clear to us at eight or nine what finally became clear to them, that they would have to play each other if they wanted competition.

Captain Van Buren, whom my father eventually came to call Van, was, the Commander said, the best player he had ever met.

"His moves are a little defensive all the time, you know, like the damn British F.O., but he knows his Sicilian, the bugger."

"Don't swear in front of the child, Commander," my mother would say, not missing a stitch in her knitting.

Ma always called him Commander. We didn't think it was odd, although it became clear that other people did. My older sister, who had been shipped back to Boston to the Ursuline Academy, had once burst into tears and wailed that she was the only girl in the world whose mother called her father by his rank instead of his name. I called him Papa until I was five and Pa after that.

"Damn fool seems surprised every time I attack him with my knights. I love to play him, love it. He doesn't learn a thing; a perfect Englishman."

When the Commander would find one of his venturesome gambits cut off and his King routed and taken, he would never admit that one can be too venturesome. To him every new idea was infallible until proven fatal.

His biggest idea, if not his worst, involved the restoration of the Manchu Dynasty and the renovation of the Great Wall of China. He tried it out on me first, explaining that it would cost about a hundred thousand dollars.

"You speak pretty good Chinese now, Neil, is that right?"

"Yes, Pa. Francis and Seiji say Gus is better, but that I'm pretty good, so I guess that means I do."

"What do you know about the royal family, Neil?"

"Not very much, Pa. Gus told me they ride around in gold carriages a lot and that the Prince of Wales isn't supposed to be very smart."

We were riding ponies out north of the city at the time. He stopped his poor pony with a yank and roared at me unmercifully. "You goddam nitwit! Not that royal family. Trouble with this country is"—he meant the United States when he said "this country"—"everyone thinks the only goddam royal family there is is that bunch of twerps over in England."

Our ponies recovered from their shock and started trotting along again.

"I mean the Manchus here. You don't by any chance play with Henry Pu Yi in that gang of yours, do you?"

It should be explained that the Commander spoke to all persons as equals except my mother. A child of ten would get exactly the same language and questions as an adult colleague. And the same angry expletives if Pa thought the answer was stupid. I was used to it, although it frightened all of my friends except Francis.

Henry Pu Yi was the little boy who was the heir to the deposed Ch'ing, or Manchu, Dynasty. He was a figure of fun to everyone. Later the Japanese would capture him and dress him up in court robes and set him up as their puppet king of Manchuria, which they called Manchukuo. Later the Chinese Communists would capture him back, the poor little pawn, and set him in the window of their revolution for whatever advertising value he had left. Our Gang had peeked over the garden wall of his family's estate once and seen him sitting in the orchard with a book in front of him, from which he absentmindedly tore a page to blow his nose.

When I think of it now, my father's idea wasn't all that different from what the Japanese and Chinese did.

"No, Pa. I saw him once, but I don't know him."

"Damn. Do any of those kids you pal around with know him?"

"I don't think so, Pa."

"Well, find out. Listen, I've got an idea that's worth a million dollars."

He was off. Even the pony put his ears forward, out of range.

"If we could ever figure out how to get the Manchus back in charge here—well, why not, someone has to be?—and this bunch of lunatics running around calling themselves a government ain't going to accomplish anything—damn Japs are going to come in here and clean 'em up—and if we could get young Henry—that's a baptismal name, find out for me if he's a Catholic or Protestant, it would be nice if he was a Catholic."

"Sure, Pa." Sure, Pa. The countryside rolled on past us and Pa went right on spouting. North of Peking is pretty in fall. Peking's in the same latitude as Boston, and the fall weather is a lot like New England. The loess and dust from the Gobi starts blowing yellow about then, and it has a sharp edge to it. Pa had given me the new sheepskin jacket I was wearing that day, and the collar was rubbing softly against my earlobes. But I didn't dare pull my head down into it and shut out Pa's voice completely.

". . . that boy on the throne, wouldn't he be grateful to us?"

I must have missed some. "Sure, Pa."

"You betcha. And do you know what I want him to do?"

"What, Pa?"

"He's a Manchu, isn't he? They're all Manchus, aren't they, his whole family? That's why they made every poor son of a bitch in China wear a pigtail for three hundred years, so they wouldn't feel homesick. Like Germans and sauerkraut. *They* don't want any wall between them and their own country, why should they?"

The Germans?

"But they aren't going to waste time tearing the damn thing down, are they? Too long. That wall would stretch from Boston to Detroit if you put it down at home. So it just sits there, falling apart. Neil, do you realize that the Great Wall of China is the only manmade thing on earth big enough to see from Mars?"

Sounded reasonable to me.

"I have a plan to shave it down into a long series of ramps. Maybe one to two miles long each. A grade of about one in eight. Get it? Graded launchers, really. Feel that damn wind?"

We stopped our ponies and watched the yellowing sky.

"For a million years that wind has swept down off Siberia. The Chinese built the Wall to stop the Mongols, and it worked, but they couldn't stop the weather. Ever think of that? This is what they call a two-coat night coming."

"You want to build it high enough to stop the wind from blowing, Pa?"

"No. Impractical damn idea if I ever heard one. What I'm going to do, if these numskulls will listen to me, is cut up about twenty miles of the Wall into two-mile-long sections, then just grade her down from northwest to southeast, see? Then we'll build a pipeline up each long ramp. Say sixteen-inch, twenty-inch copper pipe, so it won't rust. Put gigantic blast furnaces at the foot of each ramp. Hell, maybe make steel, too, but funnel the effluent heat and gases into the pipeline. Now, what have we got? We've got twenty giant heaters. Think of the cumulative energy being released. Do you know that the South American Indians make rain by building huge brush fires in dry weather? Fact. Jesuit missionary wrote about it. We could make it rain all over north China any time we wanted. Blow the damn wind right back over the Gobi if we figure out how to do that, water it and make it the biggest damn garden in Asia. Imagine that. You think the Manchus would go for that?"

"I don't know, Pa."

"Well, I'm going to ask 'em. I wonder if Van would know where they keep that little Henry. Goddam Limeys probably have him for themselves until they can put him back in the palace working for them. Goddam royalty stick together like glue. How come we can't get these so-called Chinese Republicans to do what we tell them? Just because we've got a Democrat in the White House now?"

That was news to me. I knew more about Chinese dynastic politics than I did what went on in Washington, D.C.

"Bunch of ingrates. Look at that wind blow. Maybe a three-coat night."

China is one place Christina Rossetti had never been. I knew, because she had written that you couldn't see the wind.

Pa had given me for my ninth birthday a copy of Professor Charles Franklin Brooks's book *Why the Weather*. Professor Brooks taught science at Clark University in Worcester, Massachusetts, which seemed to me a place exceptionally hospitable to eccentrics. They were the first place in America to invite Freud over to lecture. And they had another science teacher named Goddard who had shown Pa how he could fire a solid fuel rocket to a tremendous height from a tripod in his yard. Pa loved Goddard's rocket, but he loved Brooks's book even better. Naturally, it was about the weather. Better, Brooks admired Pa. He had written on the flyleaf of my birthday present: "For Neil Kelly. May you become as good a weather scientist as your Dad. Professor Charles Franklin Brooks, PhD (Harvard)."

The Commander had drilled me on that little textbook until I suppose I knew as much meteorology as any Clark graduate, at least. What Pa never knew was that I looked most often at the poem by Christina Rossetti quoted on page six:

> Who hath seen the wind?
> Neither you nor I.
> But when the trees bow down their heads
> The wind is passing by.

That poem in that book probably did as much to open me up to poetry as anything in the world. I thought it was the most wonderful thing I had ever read, and I read it over and over, trying to understand how it worked.

We rode back into the city with Pa already planning to write to some people in Europe about his new scheme.

He boasted to everyone of his "worldwide network of correspondents." The phrase became an in-joke among his colleagues. But he kept abreast of meteorological developments around the world by mail.

He knew as soon as the Norwegian press did that Tor Bergeron had done his own dry-ice experiments and induced rainfall. If he didn't find out about Findeisen in Germany for five years, it was because the new German government took its own interest in manipulating the weather and made all Findeisen's data state secrets.

When he got a letter from Veraart, the Dutchman, full of excitement about his cloud seeding, the Commander only lost heart for an hour or so, even though it knocked his hot-air pipe idea for a loop. He worked frantically over his formulae in the notebooks, checking his observations for years past, and finally, with a snap of his notebook, changed his theory by reversing it one hundred eighty degrees.

"Should have known it was cold, not heat I needed. Damn lucky I haven't got those pipes yet. No, dammit, we'll build huge ice-plants at the base of each ramp. Maybe breed buffalo out in Manchuria, bring 'em in and slaughter them once a year and freeze the meat against famine. Take the excess cold from the plants and blow it in the form of ice crystals up into the air above the Wall."

76

His new faith launched, he spent the next hour spelling out his plan to me, while I glued a model of the *Constitution* together on the table. Ma knitted in her chair by the floor lamp.

He was able to salvage a good chunk of his hot-air theory by standing that on its head, too. It dawned on him that he hadn't really been wrong, just looking at the data through the wrong end of the theodolite, so to speak.

During the course of a party at the British Embassy for the King's birthday, with plenty of Beefeater gin and Glenlivet inside all the adult guests and the kids all stuffed with macaroons, Pa got the ear of the senior air officer and explained how burning barrels of fuel oil around an airfield would enable them to dissipate fog and allow planes to land when otherwise they could not.

The British colonel, who had a chinless face with an enormous ginger moustache, peered at him with bewildered interest.

"How many barrels would it take, my dear fellow?"

"We won't know until we try, will we?"

"Rather more like fifty? Or one hundred? Not anything like one thousand, I suppose."

Pa knew the value of vagueness. "More or less, probably depends."

"Ah, I see."

"Now suppose you are coming in from Hong Kong in your plane, but the airport is fogged in."

"It has happened, my dear fellow, it has happened!"

"You see? Now, you're low on gas—petrol—and you have important news for the ambassador that you don't dare trust to the telephone."

"Oh, dear."

"What would it be worth to you to have a clear field to land on?"

"Still, stuff costs sixpence per barrel, you know. Five cents, your money. Jolly dear."

"Well, if it even took a hundred barrels—I'm not saying it would take anything like that, mind you—what would it have cost you to get your news to the ambassador in time?" The snake-oil salesman always knows that you let the customer do the final calculation, so that he thinks it's his own discovery.

"Well, er, I suppose it would cost about a pound. Five dollars your money. Be rather worth it, what?"

" 'Course, we'd have to experiment, see the best positions for the barrels, and so on."

"Oh, my dear Commander, I understand perfectly. I'll tell you what . . ." And the poor excited boob wrote out permission for my father to have access to the oil storage area at the British air depot and added a note ordering the commanding officer to assist him with work parties and materials for the experiment.

It's a short story. The Commander ringed the airfield with oil drums, and drew up a plan to ignite first each twentieth barrel, then, if that didn't clear the fog, each tenth one, and so on, down to each one. The English soldiers who sweated the oil drums into place first here, then there, then back to here, clearly thought he was insane, but probably no more than their own officers.

When the fog came after three weeks of waiting, and with it the time for the experiment, it took all the barrels. Six thousand. It wasn't so much the three hundred dollars, but that was the whole supply of fuel the British had, and there was a lot of calling back and forth between the two embassies, and closed-door inquiries, and wiring back to London and Washington before it quieted down. We never saw the chinless colonel again.

My father was jubilant. He had proved that you could dissipate fog with enough heat. He explained it again and again to Francis over a game of chess. By then he had discovered that Francis, not the captain, was the best chess player he knew.

Francis laughed and applauded each time the story was told. "Oh, Neil," he said to me, "the Commander showed them all. Really, he showed them all." I was glad for Pa's sake that at least his adopted son gave him the kind of support he never got from me.

10

TUESDAY MORNING AFTER the christening, the call came from Francis. I must remember to call him Li Chen.

"Neil, ah, good. I have spoken with Gus again, and he can come up to London on Friday. I say, is that good for you?"

He was sounding more British than the royal family now.

"I was sure it was the prime minister's butler. Where did you get that Mayfair accent, my oriental friend?"

He giggled, but didn't offer to defend it.

"Friday's fine, since, as I told you, I'm free every evening —except for my scholar's conscience, which is on its last legs anyway. When and where?"

"Sevenish? Do you know the Legation Hotel on Queen's Gate? I thought that sounded rather appropriate for our reunion, eh?"

"I can find it. I thought Queen's Gate was all Middle Eastern embassies now."

"Almost. That's one thing which makes the Legation so convenient. My own embassy likes to think that I spend a great deal of time conferring with—ah, how does one put it?—our aligned Islamic friends. Which I shall do, to a very limited extent. Their rear entrance leads to that of the Legation Hotel. *Voilà*."

"You were always a tricky little devil when it came to sneaking around Peking; I see you haven't changed. I hope, if it's an Arab hotel, they serve something stronger than orange juice."

"Oh, Neil, you droll fellow. Yes, yes, we will have drinks aplenty. The hotel is a sort of island of middle-class European tourists. I think most of them like the exoticism of the neighborhood, a sort of Kensington Casbah, y'know, with

Arabs brushing their teeth with twigs on the sidewalk and that sort of wog thing."

"I'll be there. If you're not, I'll know your government has found out about that back exit and you're back home with another placard around your neck. In the bar?"

"Yes, yes. The bar, downstairs. A terrible bar. No one ever goes there, so we will have it to ourselves."

Queen's Gate was close enough to the Victoria and Albert that it was familiar territory for me. Any American who has been to London on a study grant gets to know the Borough of Kensington and Russell Square, by the British Museum, better than any other parts of the city.

The Legation was a modest, quiet establishment, which, when I entered the lobby, was catering to a large contingent of Irish schoolboys who had just disembarked from a super-bus out front. I edged through their polite, patient ranks past the counting finger of their schoolmaster and went down to the bar.

Francis and Gus were together in easy chairs around a small table in the back of the half-dark room. Except for the young woman in the black wig and immense false eyelashes tending the bar and reading *Time Out*, there was no one else.

I greeted them across the room and stopped at the bar for a bottle of Guinness.

Gus edged another low chair into a tight circle around the table. "Neil, sit."

"Welcome, Neil."

"Sorry if I'm a little late. I turned the wrong way coming out of the Gloucester Road station."

"Francis has been telling me about his meteoric rise and fall and resurrection in the People's Republic. Fascinating."

"I'm glad you're having as much trouble as I am remembering his new name. I promise you, Francis, I'll keep on trying."

He laughed good-naturedly. "It will seem normal to you after a while. I was at first myself like a new bride. Sometimes I didn't remember myself and I had to look in my checkbook to see who I was."

Francis had successively enjoyed success and suffered defeat in a way that was probably normal for a lot of Chinese intellectuals and businessmen during the years after 1945. He had been smart or lucky enough to attach himself to the Maoists after it became apparent that even American support could not keep Chiang K'ai Shek's rickety Kuomintang in power for long. He told us that many of his cousins had been on the Long March, and I teased him about that.

"Come, Francis, not your cousins the Soongs, surely. They were running all the banks in Shanghai."

He looked delighted at my comment. "That is true, Neil. But of course I have a great many cousins. Even the great Madame Soong, who was the widow of our George Washington, Sun Yat Sen, became a vice-president of the Mao government, you know. So them too, them too." He giggled hysterically and spilled his drink on himself and, brushing it off, spilled more. His accent lost some of its BBC fruitiness as he drank and gossipped.

He had finally been sent by his family to Tsinghua University, the so-called MIT of China, just northwest of Peking. There he had, of all things, studied meteorology, and had eventually become one of China's foremost weather scientists.

"So you see how much I owe your father the Commander, Neil. Because of the training he gave this little Chinese boy in observation and meteorological history and all that, I was able to begin very early reading science."

He leaned forward and put his hand to his mouth, talking through his fingers. "In China, I must be frank to admit to you, my friends, we are far, far behind the west in science." He held up one finger. "One aneroid barograph we had, and one old boxed Fortin mercury barometer, a hair hygrograph, yes, you would not believe it?, and one theodolite, just one of each thing. And we are still not even, you must know. I am so embarrassed to tell you this, but W. N. Shaw, *Manual of Meteorology*, 1926, translated into Chinese by

Li Chen, was our basic text! I am talking about 1965. Your father, Neil, that great, good man, gave me that book. I said on the dedication page of my translation: *To the Commander*. They thought I meant Mao, of course, so they left it. It was used against me later, though, when they accused me of dedicating it to Lin Piao, the traitor, who was also called Commander by some factions. I said to them 'What does Lin Piao know about the weather?' That was used against me, too. They said it sounded Confucian, evasive and feudal." He threw up his hands. "I ask you. Gnomic utterance is a dangerous pastime among zealots. The Sermon on the Mount they understand; the Revelations of St. John, not."

"But you survived," Gus said drily.

"Did I not? But first I was greeted as a prodigy. You will enjoy this, Neil. I was made a professor of meteorological science at Tsinghua as soon as I took my degree. Oh, yes. I wanted to go to Cal Tech, you see, where the greatest long-range meteorologists in the world are. Or to Cambridge, Gus. Very brilliant sciences at Cambridge, as we all know. But China needed the few of us there were, so I became Professor Li Chen."

"Are you still a Christian, Li Chen?" Gus asked him, puffing to light his pipe.

"Of course, my friends, of course I am. Why not? Oh, you have probably heard that all government officials must officially be atheists. I think there was something like that here in England in Queen Elizabeth's time. The first Elizabeth, to be sure. One had to swear, and many good men said, 'Oh, yes, I am this, Your Majesty, and not that,' and they went right on being what they were. Is that not so?"

Perhaps Donne.

Gus grunted. "Some surely did. Some died rather than say it."

"Oh, what foolish fellows they were. You can bet none of them was Chinese."

"As a matter of fact," I put in, "the book I am trying to

write is about one fellow, a poet, who did change his coat, and eventually ceased to be a poet."

"Well of course, the foolish fellow," Francis said indignantly. "Of course he did. We will all make a rule, we three. The rule of Li Chen, like the American Law of Murphy, eh? You must change your shirt many times, but you must not change your coat at all."

The third round of drinks was getting to us; we all sounded sillier to me.

Gus objected in his pleasantly quarrelsome way. "Shouldn't the rule be the other way around? Shouldn't you change your coat often—change on the outside, you see—but not your shirt? Or at least your vest, your undershirt, as you Yanks call it."

Francis applauded the revision. "Yes, yes. That is it. The committee of three has amended the motion. Not your undershirt. My undershirt, the undershirt of old chum Francis Li, is still Christian. The garment of my baptism, you see. Soon, who knows, that might be a fashionable garment again. China is publishing an encyclopedia of world religions, you know. As a lowly minister of culture, I was even asked to advise on the Catholic section. Oh, they know that I still have my Catholic undershirt, yes."

"Perhaps *sub specie aeternitatis*, Francis," I said to him jokingly, "your undershirt is still as white as snow. You may certainly hope so."

"What is this? Latin? Greek? You know, Neil, I do not know these foreign languages of the old west—no, it is not the old west, is it, that is Wyoming and so on. What does this mean, then?"

"It means under the eye of God, Francis. From the point of view provided by eternal, not merely temporal considerations."

He put his hands to his fat cheeks and rocked back and forth. "Oh, some of my temporal considerations have been most unfortunate indeed."

Francis had fared badly during the Cultural Revolution. Tsinghua University was where it all started among Chinese students, and at the height of the brawling and strikes in 1967, our old chum had been sacked and banished to the rural hinterlands for some corrective manual labor.

"Tsinghua was far worse than Columbia or California, you know, Neil. Many of us on the faculty were accused by People's Courts—which meant, of course, our students—of forgetting the truth of Mao in favor of Lin Piao or some other deviationist devil. Some of the students set off on a kind of Children's Crusade through the city, bullying people in restaurants and in shops; the rest became our judges. It was, you know, much more fun for them than studying.

"We were all declared guilty. All of us. Off to the farms. I pulled a night-soil cart for two years. You know what that is? Yes, terrible stink, very hard work. Collecting human shit and taking it out to the fields. We have too few farm animals in China to make enough shit for all the land, you know, but plenty of human shit."

He giggled and applauded himself. The girl at the bar reading *Time Out* looked shocked, but uncapped more beer at Gus's signal.

"But in good time, all was made right. I got tremendous muscles, which had been getting fat—you see, I need punishment now, I am very fat again, eh?—and they asked me not to go back to my old position, but to become a junior minister of culture and international affairs. Not so junior now, very nearly in charge of the whole shooting match, eh? And now I am in London, doing some international affairs. Very hard work. The British, Gus, are very formidable in international affairs, because they have had so much experience."

I asked him, if he was a government minister, why he had to sneak out back doors of Arab embassies to meet a couple of old friends for a beer.

"Oh, Neil, tsk, tsk. Surely you know the answer to that. And you, Gus, my old British chum, yes?"

Francis paused, then drank his beer carefully, squinting at us crookedly through his cigarette smoke.

"Tell us, Francis, old Chinese chum."

"But they think you two are spies. One American, one British spy." He spread his hands apart helplessly.

Gus snorted through his pipe. "Do you?"

"Do I think you are spies? I think I will let you tell me. I think you would not lie to an old boy from Our Gang."

I raised my right hand. "Not me, Francis."

Gus solemnly did the same and belched. "Not me. Sorry."

Francis giggled and coughed on his smoke, brushing ashes from his jacket. "You see? A kind of paradox. If you are spies, you must say that. Does that prove it or not? We have a Lewis Carroll situation here."

I fanned his smoke away. Between the two of them they were creating enough pollution to cause cancer on the spot.

"Francis, that's the most paranoid thing I ever heard."

"Oh, Neil, my smoke is bothering you. I am so sorry." He kept right on smoking, but now waved at the air every few words. "Chinese paranoia is quite different from yours. When a westerner is paranoid, he thinks his friends are his enemies. The Russians are never so European as when they are feeling paranoid. Trotsky swore, you know, that Stalin himself was actually a Czarist spy. Stalin accused his foreign minister, Molotov, of being an agent of British intelligence. Beria, chief spymaster of the Soviet Union, was denounced as a foreign agent. Unfortunately they all died. It goes on and on.

"Now we Chinese know our friends and we know our enemies. When we go mad—crazy, you know—it takes the form of simple xenophobia in its germinal stage. Hating foreigners is what you would call a warm-up. Then it becomes a form of heightened consciousness of reality. Really, don't laugh. Chinese insanity is more like western religious mysticism than anything else. Our saints are our political leaders and scientists. We live so close to the edge of reality, you see, with so few layers of insulation between us and it, that it cuts us like knives. We are mad with ecstasy then, and the world simply calls us mad. But it is the truth we are drunk with. Not Mai-tai or anything like that. Not like this good beer we drink."

He sat back and beamed at us.

Good old Gus was a veteran of too many all-night bull sessions with drunken English undergraduates, who are the most ardent and fluent bullshitters in the world, to let him get away with a speech like that.

"You're talking absolute cock, you know, Francis."

"No, Gus, not absolute cock, as you say. The test is pragmatic, is it not? Something good we learned from the American philosophers, Neil. What is good is so because it works and will be kept. What fails will be swept away. We shall have to see what works, that is all."

"But you can't do that." I was indignant, but not feeling terribly articulate. Undergraduate nonsense is one thing, but here was a responsible official of a great power tossing off a principle as deadly as any you could frame, *if* it were applied to human beings. "You can't just try anything, using human beings as guinea pigs, and then count the bodies and say, 'Okay, that wasn't such a good idea, let's not try that again. Let's try this instead.' "

"But Neil, doesn't America conduct its whole foreign policy that way?"

"It might look that way sometimes, and with this damned administration we've got now—"

"And the one before that? And before that?"

Gus intervened hotly. "Come off it, Francis. You are a government minister. We are just a couple of poor blokes trying to stay afloat, voting our consciences, not power brokers or policy makers. You're the one who must answer for it if you launch a program of ethical nihilism, not us."

"How well the British know about that, eh, Gus? The British Empire was surely the great annihilator all over Asia and Africa, were they not? You are still hanging on to the scraps, too, like the Chinese city of Hong Kong, eh?"

I reminded him that he had once told me that if he could not be Chinese, he would rather be British than anything else, including American.

"It is true!" He clapped his hands. "I have such a nostalgia for the old monarchies, you know. Quite disgraceful for a Communist. Not for the bloody Manchus, you know,

86

those foreign devils, but for the Ming, the last great pure Chinese dynasty, which was unhappily eradicated at about the time of your Shakespeare and your John Donne and Queen Elizabeth, you know. 'The Brilliant.' Few foreigners know that 'Ming' means that. Glorious, oh, yes, if I could not be Chinese, Neil, I should much prefer to be British."

Gus winked at me. "I can see that," he said thoughtfully. "If I weren't British, I should want to be British, too."

11

I WAS DISTURBED by that reunion with Francis. I listened to his blithe words and thought about the boy I had known and the man he was now.

I have no liking for ideologues of any kind: cold men who center their lives in some abstraction or other—science, or politics, or scholarship, for that matter—and give up their full, imperfect humanity for the imagined excellence of the world of ideas. Only half the suffering in the world is caused by unfeeling stupidity; the rest is caused by unfeeling intelligence. And too often the stupid are put to work for the smart, doing their evil for them. Poor dumb soldiers thrilled to be burning out a village, children on a pointless crusade, or thugs breaking their victim's arms and legs because some Don or some two-bit warlord in an expensive suit has pointed his finger.

When my old playmate spoke casually of experimenting with history to see what worked, as though populations were counters, my blood chilled. I hammered at him about it, wishing I had not drunk so much Guinness, but he was as cute and elusive as a monkey, just as he had been in Our Gang.

"Dammit, Francis, or Li Chen or whatever shirt you're wearing now, you can't talk about experimenting with the lives of your own people. Or even with the lives of your neighbors on the planet. They are us."

"But, but, but Neil, be reasonable. That is what it requires to have progress. As for people, we have more than enough. How many had to die after 1949, Neil? Just to get the land away from the greedy landlords and into the hands of the farmers who do the work? Some twenty-six million, my friend. More or less, you know. Think of that number, how large. But they were parasites. The farmers would have had to die if the landlords did not. So, which was better? Obviously, one must kill the parasites."

"One musn't," Gus barked, "arbitrarily kill anyone. You can't just decide this group or that group has to go and eliminate them."

"Oh, yes, Gus. We can. We did, you see. I am not in the least embarrassed, either. How many children did you both see in Peking in the old days with deformed arms and legs and big swollen bellies? How many dead men and women did the carts pick up in the cold months, or how many just lay there being gnawed by the flies and the rats? Hundreds of millions, all over China. Their crime was to be poor, and they were poor because they had no land. Now Peking is free of human filth. Do try to remember the smell there. And the flies—do you remember how they would be caked on the beggars and on the food in the stalls, on the children's eyes? Now, none. None. You would not even recognize your old Peking now."

We argued on, going back and forth, for another hour. Now, even in retrospect, the arguments Francis made sicken me. But so did the vivid memories he recalled. The human garbage of the alleys being shoveled into carts, the diseased beggar children edging away fearfully from our mob of protected little princes, protected by our wealth and our parents' positions, and by the color of our skins, Gus and I.

"Two thousand new Chinese every hour, even taking the death rate into account, Neil," Francis said. "Since we have been talking here tonight, old friends in London, perhaps five thousand new mouths to feed. Would you have us *not* experiment with better ways to do it?"

We finally turned the conversation around one hundred eighty degrees, to what Gus and I had been doing since leaving Peking at different times in 1937. Gus and I knew some of each other's story, because we had met once during the war, but Francis was eager to hear all of it.

It was the famous Kelly family "hot appendix," which I had

allegedly inherited from my dissolute paternal grandfather, that ended my active seagoing career almost before it started, but also made it possible for me to run into Gus in Hawaii.

Because there seemed little point in starting college when I graduated from Efford High School in the June of 1942, I told my mother at supper graduation night that I would be joining the navy the next day.

She shook her head silently and kept on eating in her picky, birdy way and cried a little, also silently. I had graduated valedictorian of my class—not a very remarkable feat at Efford High, where most of my classmates were the children of Italian laborers, bent either on getting a job in the Navy Yard to avoid the draft or joining the army. After the Commander's death we had settled there because Ma had a cousin in business nearby who could take her on as a counter clerk in his variety store, and me as a delivery boy for eight dollars a week.

Ma and I never argued; I wished sometimes that we could. The navy had me on a train to Newport for basic training in ten days. At seventeen there was no way I could be an officer unless I applied for one of the V-5 or V-12 programs, but V-5 was flying, in which I had no interest, and I knew the other one was just the navy's quick solution to training up a bunch of know-nothing ensigns who would stand in the front end of landing craft and say "Follow me" when they hit the beaches.

At Newport they asked little of me but a willingness to do callisthenics for six weeks and memorize the ten general orders. When it came time to be tested for specialist training, it was even easier than at Efford to top the class. Most of the men in my barracks were the sons of Polish laborers from Bayonne, New Jersey, anxious to qualify as gunner's mates or mechanics. I was the only applicant for Aerographer's School, the navy's name for Weather School, and I was transferred to Lakewood, New Jersey, the week after I finished boot camp.

The school, which the navy ingloriously called ASTU, Aerographers School Training Unit, and which had been the Cardinal Newman Preparatory School before that went bankrupt, was entirely unmilitary. Over the front door was inscribed the Newman motto, *Cor Ad Cor Loquitur*, and we attended lectures on meteorology in ordinary, familiar classrooms.

"This is easy for you, Kelly, isn't it?" the lieutenant commander who read our exam papers said to me in his office one day.

"So far, sir."

"Did you study meteorology in high school, Kelly?"

"No, sir." I sighed inwardly, but admitted it. "My father was a navy meteorologist, sir. He made me memorize Shaw's 1926 *Manual*, both volumes, chapter by chapter, before I was twelve."

"Your father? That so?"

So much for old navy ties in the mind of the new. He couldn't have replied more absentmindedly if I had said that my father was a middle-aged man.

"Would you like to stay here in the school as an instructor when you finish the course, Kelly? Pierce First says you know as much as he does."

A duck knew as much as Waldo Pierce, Aerographer's Mate First Class.

"It would mean promoting you to Second Class the week after you make Third, but Pierce says you'll be First as soon as we let you take the test anyway, so . . ."

It was time to stop this pipe dream. Spending the war in Lakewood, New Jersey, was someone's dream of heaven, but not mine.

"If it's all right with you, sir—I mean, thank you, Commander, but I'd much rather go to sea."

He looked astonished, doused it. Civilian to his marrow, he seemed to shudder at the thought himself.

"That will be all, then, Kelly. We certainly don't want anyone at the school who doesn't want to be. You know our motto."

"Yes, sir. *Cor Ad Cor Loquitur*. 'Heart speaketh unto heart.' "

"Not quite. 'We Serve in All Weather.' Not official, of course, my own suggestion for the school. Hasn't had final approval from Washington yet. I'm sure you'll find plenty of men at sea who'd give a great deal for this duty, demanding as it is. Dismissed."

So I was assigned to a newly launched escort carrier, the *Alikula Bay*, and we were outward bound on a shakedown cruise to Hawaii when my appendix flared up. They carried me off the ship at Ford Island and put me into sick bay for an emergency appendectomy. By the time it was out and I was up, the *Alikula Bay* was under weigh back to San Diego, and my papers had been pulled for reassignment to Weather Central, Fleet Headquarters, CINCPAC, Honolulu.

It was one of the plums of navy duty then. A lot of spit and polish with all those admirals around, but not a war zone and

Waikiki Beach down the street, reserved for us, any time we wanted it.

When the Personnel Officer found out I could read Japanese and Chinese, he almost had an orgasm. When they pushed harder and found out I could read Japanese weather codes, they thought they had struck gold in the old mill stream.

"You're a freak, Kelly. A beautiful frigging freak," Captain Jackson said, saluting me.

"There's a problem, sir," the P.O., an ensign, said to the captain.

"My ass. Assign him to Special Section, F.W.C."

The ensign smiled coldly and waited for a chance to finish. "Impossible, Captain."

The captain's neck swelled and he turned dark red. "Goddammit, Hofstadter, whatever it is, forget it. It just ceased to exist. Rectify it. File the goddam problem under 'solved' and forget it. I want this kid in Special Section."

Mr. Hofstadter was at ease with loud captains. I discovered later it was because his family owned Ford Island, on which we were all standing, and was leasing it to the U.S. Navy for a quarter of a million dollars a year.

"Then you'd better get your boss to commission him. You know the goddam standing order as well as I do, Captain: no one below the rank of ensign in special section. Christ, Captain, they need a CPO just to deliver the coffee to the door over there."

"Well, what a load of shit that is, Hofstadter," was the best rebuttal the captain could manage. He looked at me. "How old are you, Kelly?"

"Seventeen, sir."

"Jesus. And you already know two oriental languages? You some kind of a child prodigy?"

"I grew up in Asia, sir, speaking Chinese. The written languages are basically the same."

"Damn. That right? I wonder if Nimitz knows that. You look about fifteen. How the hell can I make a kid like you an ensign?"

I sighed inwardly again and said what I had said back in Lakewood, New Jersey.

"May I say something, sir?"

He shrugged. Another ninety-day officer who never would really be Navy. My father would have loved him. "I'd rather keep

92

my present rank and go back to sea if I could be assigned to a new ship."

He looked at me as if I were insane. "Don't be an asshole, Kelly." His eyes narrowed and his voice got hard and I could see the iron behind the hearty bluff. "If you went back on sea duty now, it would probably be someplace like Kiska or Attu, up in the goddam Aleutians, where it sleets sideways ten months a year. You don't want that, son, do you? And Mr. Hofstadter here, he wouldn't want to write those orders either, would he?"

It was called being shanghaied.

"Hoffy, you miserable excuse for an officer, call Pratt over there in Aiea and tell him this situation. This boy here needs a new set of papers cut immediately, Hof. Lost his other goddam papers when he got transferred to sick bay. Tell that old bastard Kelly here is twenty-one—stand a little taller, for Chrissakes, Kelly, will you, if you want people to believe you're twenty-one?—and I want him commissioned an ensign ASAP and get him a suit with a gold stripe on it and get his tender young ass over to Special Section by 0800 hours Monday."

He put a fatherly arm around my shoulders. "Admiral Pratt's my man. After this goddam war he and I are going into business together to sell portable weather stations and landing fields to the army. I'll be his boss then. Listen." He sat down on a chair straddling it and put his huge finger on my chest. "You're only a goddam enlisted man, so I'm not telling you this—Hofstadter, get the hell out into the galley while I talk to this man, will you, for Chrissakes?—but when you're an officer and a gentleman and a few years older next Monday, remember this and think about it in between."

What he told me was that in the Special Section of Fleet Weather Central they were intercepting a flood of Japanese coded radio transmissions. For which they had the key. "That's the big hot tamale, Kelly. We know the bastards' code!" Tens of thousands of messages were piling up, and there weren't enough cryptographers in Washington or linguists in Hawaii with navy rank to read the results. He wanted me to take a desk and, starting Monday, read Japanese transmissions as fast as they were decoded to sort out the weather information from the rest.

"There's a goddam long war ahead out there, Kelly; we not only have to build the damn ships and man them, we have to sail

93

them up the goddam Pacific island by island and take back everything from the Gilberts to the China coast. And do you know what we have out there right now to give us weather information on that stretch of ocean? This is top secret classified goddam information, Kelly, and I'll cut your tongue out if you say you got it from me. We've got one—*one*—goddam submarine out there surfacing every once and a while to bat out a weather report, then diving again before the whole Jap navy sails down their periscope. That's more square miles of ocean than whores in Panama City, boy, and we got just one little feller to satisfy them all. Plain stupid."

"You want me to pick off the Japanese weather-ship reports."

"Now you're talking. I like you, Kelly, smart bastard. You'll field their reports and we'll use them to forecast for our side. Beautiful?"

It took a lot more doing than Captain Jackson thought, but that's exactly what we did over the next three years.

And that's why I was stationed in Fleet Headquarters, Pacific, when Gus Van Duren walked through the door in 1944.

12

LIKE ME, GUS was attached to an admiral because of his Asian languages. Unlike me, his family connections and his imposing intelligence had provided him with a commission right out of Winchester.

I had taken Bill Speller's O.D. duty at the BOQ so that he could go see his girlfriend, a Japanese-Hawaiian girl he preferred not to bring onto the base. I was engaged in the exciting navy maneuver called supply inventory, linen, and the voice was familiar before I could even lift my eyes from the laundry list I was checking. We were twenty-six pillowcases short.

"Leftenant Austin Van Duren reporting for temporary assignment to quarters, sir. Good God: Neil."

I jumped up, spilling my coffee all over my laundry list in my excitement, and grabbed his hand.

"Gus, you old bastard."

"God, look who they've created an officer."

We whacked each other on the backs and mopped up coffee and explained the terribly important activity the supply officer had left me with and saluted each other a couple of times, both talking at once, both finally stopping at once to say, "You first."

"Tin shoo po yaw."

"I say. Our mother tongue."

Fresh laughs, fresh babble at cross-purposes. I think we were both surprised at how emotional a meeting it was. Neither of us was the demonstrative type.

While I fixed him up with visitor's privileges, he explained his arrival in Honolulu. Reduced to its simples, the Brits wanted their navy in on the Pacific campaign on equal terms with the Americans.

"You people can't afford it, Gus."

"Chum, my boss is telling your boss, even as we speak here amid the sheets and pillowcases, that we can't afford to be left out. Too much to lose when everyone settles up in Asia if we aren't here too."

"Come on, Gus. England needs every damn ship and gun she can get in the Channel, true or false?"

He paused in laying out his kit in a bedside locker. "Neil, England is standing on the last inch. Gray as ashes. London. You wouldn't believe it. Exeter, for God's sake, wrecked. Plymouth doesn't even exist anymore. It's as though the Vandals—the original ones—had come through and beaten it all flat."

"Then what the hell do you want to take half your fleet away from there for and bring it over here? It makes no sense."

"Actually, only a token squadron. Different point of view, Neil. There's still a lot of empire this side of Suez, y'know, and we invested a good deal in getting it. India, Singapore, Hong Kong ..."

"Well, my boss is telling your boss right now not to worry. We'll have it all back for you by forty-eight at the latest, gift wrapped."

"Is that the current betting? Forty-eight?" He stretched out on the cot luxuriously. "I could sleep till then. But I need a shower. And a large drink."

"I'll take you for a swim. Let the Waikiki waves massage your tired bones and all will be well. Next best thing to the love of a loyal woman. Then dinner at the Moana on me."

"Not yet." He struggled to a sitting position and began stripping off his soiled uniform. "We rally our forces at 1800 hours for whatever. Fuller's determined not to let Nimitz and King squeeze us out, you know, and we have standing orders not to relax our guard while you Yanks sweet-talk us and waltz us around and get us all pissed on your dangerous American martini cocktails with ice in them."

"Promise, no ice. British paranoia, that, about the ice."

"Yes, I daresay. But remember, I've been trained for this mission by being forced to crunch ice cubes between my teeth while being interrogated by sadists."

"I swear, no ice. Ve haf oder, crueller vays off makink you talk."

"You haven't any fresh razor blades, I suppose? You do? My resistance to torture is great, but for a shave with hot water and a sharp razor I'll tell you our deepest secret."

I produced a package of Gillettes for him and he grabbed them and kissed them.

"Fuller keeps one typed sheet posted on the wardroom door. It's the remark one of your senior admirals who will be nameless, but who is now over there having drinks with him, made in a careless moment. 'The biggest favor the English can do us is keeping their goddam ships out of the Pacific altogether.' "

"Oh, that. The papers ate it up here, too. But the logic behind it is more complicated than just jealousy over whose claim this is. You know damn well that we've built a long-legged fleet and you people have always had a short-legged one."

Gus groaned. "Here it comes. That's just so much crap and you know it, Ensign Kelly."

"Fact, Gus, fact. Our supply and fuel ships run with us. You damned Brits have to put into a gas station every two hundred miles or thirty days, whichever comes first."

He waved my argument away. "We've had a navy, you know, Neil, since long before you people had a pot to piss in."

The argument roared on right through his shower, with Gus yelling colorful insults about all American naval procedures except hot showers out through the steam. We didn't drop it until an irate lieutenant commander stuck his head in and piped us down.

We eventually did get to the Moana for dinner and to the beach. The conference, which involved State Department and Senate types flown hurriedly out from Washington, and at least one Chinese general, who spent most of his time asking Gus about cricket scores, went on for ten days. Some compromise on both sides, but no joint action scheduled for the foreseeable future. Things were moving too fast by then. We were leap-frogging whole island groups by then, and had everything between the Solomons and the Marianas back, along with the staging areas we needed north of New Guinea. That meant the Philippines next, then we'd be sitting in the South China Sea.

My own readings of Japanese radio transmissions told me without any analysis what was up. Where their weather and picket ships had been patrolling, we were now patrolling.

The day after Gus and I drove out to the back beaches to see the gigantic surf, the British mission pulled out unceremoniously.

The last evening before Gus left we had a conversation that seemed a little odd later, but since we were both spiffed on icy dry martinis at the time, probably seemed as normal as everything else then.

"Are you planning to stay in the navy after the war, Neil?"

"Hell, no. I gave the U.S. Navy my childhood and my young

manhood. That's it. I haven't even been to college yet. Don't tell me you?"

"Not a bit. I want to draw and paint more than ever. If Paris is still there then, I'll probably go there to study. Rome, perhaps. Somewhere. God, no, no more RN for me."

"All I want to do is start reading something besides Japanese weather reports. I feel so ignorant."

"You're not exactly regarded as hopeless by the people on our side who've met you, y'know. Jameson, for one."

"Is he the one with the buck teeth who's as queer as Confederate money?"

"Oh, dear, he didn't fondle you, did he?"

"No, but I got the impression he was going to If I stood still."

"There's very little harm in Jamey. He's bent, but he's not aggressive about it. I rather think it was your linguistic abilities and quick intelligence he was coveting."

"Come on."

He looked down into his drink and swirled the ice. "Your name is on a list."

"What list? Whose list?"

"I'm not telling you this. You are torturing me with martinis, just as they told me in training school you would, and I am telling you things which perhaps were better left unsaid."

"Dammit, what list."

"Well, old chum, in the name of personal loyalty, and leaving king and country out of it for the moment, I'll tell you this small much. Like you, my fellow junior officer and ally, I get stuck with shitty little details like laundry lists and filing, too. I am, let me confess, pretty much the file clerk for our delegation. I wonder if there is a decoration for that?" He posed. "This splendid gong was awarded to Leftenant Van Duren for indominitable—these are very strong martini cocktails, Ensign Kelly, sir—for indominal fortitude and reckless gallantry in the face of friendly files attacking him night and day from all bloody directions of the compass. He never flinched or flunched. He—"

"Gus, I'll—"

"Yes. Well. Amongst the portfolios prepared by your side to be given to my side yesterday were listings of Asian regions, with names of personnel attached to each list. Your name appears on the China list, the Japan list, and the Korean list."

I was bewildered. "What's that supposed to mean? Am I

being offered in trade to the Brits for a couple of used mine-sweepers, or what?"

"I haven't the foggiest. Well, I do, actually, if you want a half-educated guess, since Jameson is involved. Would you like my indominabominable guess?"

He knew from my glare that I did. Someone was taking my name, and maybe my future, in vain.

"Yes, well. Can see you do. We're not planning to lose all this again, you know." He gestured drunkenly in the general direction of Asia. "When this beastly war is finished and these despicable little bastards are swept up and dumped back into their island home, the allied powers, or someone, are going to have to do a far better job of policing Asia. That. Means. Intelligence."

He put his finger on my chest and punctuated each word. "We can't wait to read in the *Singapore Times* that the Japs are up again, can we? Or perhaps the Chinese the next time, eh?"

"Do you mean that someone on my side is nominating me to your side for this postwar intelligence work? I'm going to be a peacetime spy?" The idea was so preposterous I was relieved. I was afraid someone was putting me on a late list, to be kept on in the navy when the war ended, under some emergency pretext or other.

I punctuated his chest this time. "O.U.T., Gus, that's all I want. Good-bye, farewell, aloha, so long, Yokahama mama. Neil is going home. Christina Rossetti here I come."

Gus smiled drunkenly. "Yes, hmm, I daresay. That's what they teach us to say in training school when we're too pissed to think of anything intelligent. Hmm, yes, I daresay. But Neil, my old chum, don't be wholly naive to me, will you? You do know, don't you, that your Special Services Division is a department of Naval Intelligence? They have told you that much, at least, hm?"

They hadn't, but it seemed a technicality, one of those administrative decisions that has more to do with what file drawer a piece of paper goes in than with any reality.

We went over to the Officers' Club for what proved to be our final drink together during the war. The talk was about the mammoth tits on a movie star who'd come through with a U.S.O. troupe and about baseball. Gus was very quiet the rest of the evening. I suppose he knew he would be pulling out the next day, but had been ordered not to say so.

And so my name had gone onto a list. And if Jameson had been feeling me up as a possible recruit for British Intelligence, nothing ever came of it. Or perhaps something did and I wasn't bright enough to know it.

Perhaps some of the conversations I had in college were also vettings, cryptic intercourse with OSS or CIA scouts, with someone smilingly testing my depths and angles without me ever tumbling. I certainly never heard the word "intelligence" ever used in any context except its correct one, having to do with the exercise of intellectual powers in intellectual pursuits.

Some of my classmates who appeared to drift quite naturally into positions as cultural attachés here and there proved in later years to have actual connections not with the State Department but with the CIA, but I knew none of them well.

Perhaps I slipped through the mesh in their screen, with a stamp next to my name in the dossier: WON'T DO. LIT MAJOR. LACKS ALL POLITICAL SENSE.

If I tried my damndest, I could recall only a single occasion when it seems reasonable to believe that someone, during my undergraduate days, was sounding me out about something beyond graduate school in literature.

Our baseball teams, including JV and Freshman, had gone to Cambridge on a Friday to play Harvard. Afterward—I think we lost the JV game, in which I hit for our pitcher and grounded out—there was a party at Kirkland House more or less in our honor. Many Radcliffe girls, much throwing of large objects like telephone books out of windows in the general direction of Boylston Street, a bathtub full of ice and cans of Narragansett beer, and talk flowing through several adjoining suites with their fire doors open.

Eventually we were all dancing in the Common Room. Faculty and tutors and housemasters, senior and junior, passing through. In the course of it a very senior professor was introduced to me, and ten minutes into mindless chatter about baseball and Old Hampton, I realized that he was, in addition to being a Harvard professor, a retired admiral who was engaged in writing some kind of naval history of the Pacific war.

He asked me smilingly why on earth I had chosen to go to Old Hampton instead of to Harvard. It must be understood that Old Hampton had been founded in 1761 to rival Harvard over some lost point in Congregational theology, and that the Cambridge people had never quite got over their amazement at this upstart place. My interrogator seemed genuinely concerned for my intellectual welfare out in the wilds of the Connecticut Valley.

At the time, apart from trying to play baseball, I was passing through my Waugh-character phase. I was determined to become our campus's only Anglo-Catholic literary figure. I wore tweed suits at all times, because of something on the subject that I had read in *Brideshead Revisited*: never flannels with a tweed jacket. Important things like that.

"After the rather interesting war you had, I should think you'd be wanting something more . . . demanding."

Someone had bothered to tell him I had had an interesting war. Somewhere Sebastian Flyte hugged his teddy bear and smiled.

"Exactly."

The Admiral had played right into Waugh's hands, and mine. I gestured. "I decided that one simply couldn't make an adequate career of hating Yale. Somehow it never seemed sufficiently important."

He looked at me from under one bushy eyebrow. Was this character kidding?

"There are a few more important things here."

"Oh, I suppose so. You have the former German Chancellor, don't you, the Centrist? And the last Menshevik Commissar of Justice under Kerensky. I suppose one could meet most of the famous refugees of our time in Cambridge eventually if one set about it assiduously."

I don't recall that we pursued the question. Could I have been put down on another list, as a hopeless pansy? Harvard prides itself on its wit, but actually, I've always found it deficient in that respect at the really important, spiritual level.

13

IT WAS 1937, in the spring, and I was twelve when the Commander finally was granted an audience in the lair of the old liar Backhouse, at 19 Shih-Fuma Street in Tartar City. Outside the green doors with their vermilion lozenges bearing the names of the Confucian virtues in black, after much negotiation of gratuities, we were permitted to meet and talk with the hermit-scholar and friend of kings.

I was terrified. Pa did not know that I had, on at least a dozen occasions, stood on the roadside and shouted "Pee Yew!" at this eminent scholar and literary lion. While I waited for Sir Edmund, W.C., to realize it and have me fried in oil, I trembled in my boots.

He did not seem to recognize me. Perhaps he had never even noticed us. It was a disappointment and a relief.

The Hermit of Peking listened to the Commander's lecture on China's weather, making several knowledgeable comments about the drought and flood conditions of the early empires and crop declines over the past century, and stroked his white beard and, in the kindliest way, offered me ginger candy.

The talk went on and on. I had heard at least half of it many times before. This particular presentation, in which Pa importuned Sir Edmund to intercede with the remaining family of the Dowager Empress Tzu Hsi, whose lover all Peking believed him to have been, was about making ice ramps out of the Great Wall.

What Pa would never know, and what no one but the old lion himself knew then, was that Backhouse was to prove the biggest fraud of the century. He must have sat there listening to the old snake-oil salesman in the American navy uniform and silently admired a brother con man. Perhaps he wondered about going into business as partners. Pa had never been more mellifluous. Even I almost believed some of what he said.

The old man's absorbed interest drove the Commander to new heights of improvisation. He added to his litany a claim I, at least, had never heard before.

"I don't know how to put this, Sir Edmund. You understand, of course, that everything we are discussing here must be held in the strictest confidence."

Sir Edmund reassured him with a magisterial gesture.

"If my government were to know," the Commander said, low voiced, "they might see it as an indiscretion amounting to more than forgivable carelessness, if you get me."

The old intriguer assured him that he got him very well.

Pa paused. His secret was being pulled out of him by fate or forces far beyond his power to resist. "There is a formula."

The white beard wagged. "I see. A formula."

"My own."

"Ah."

"We live at the bottom of an ocean of air, you know."

The old man looked bewildered. The Commander had thrown him a spitball. "Indeed?"

"I have studied the surface of that ocean."

"You fly, Commander?"

"My kites fly, Sir Edmund. The kites of my Chinese kitemaker by appointment to the American legation, I should say. A genius of aeronautical dynamics. And, by the way, a cousin of the Li family and also of the Soongs."

Francis's uncle Mathew.

"What does one learn up there at the surface, Commander?"

Pa paled a little and breathed slowly. I once saw a movie in which a Swedish actress had a baby by natural childbirth; Pa looked like that woman then. "The final clue necessary to perfect weather prediction over a long range." He paused for a sensation, didn't get it, so went right on selling. "There are, sir, atop our sea of air, as on the surface of the ocean, currents, waves, and swells. As surely as one can learn to tell the sea in terms of its fetch, its changes of movement, its ups and downs, to put the matter simply, and predict its eventual rages and calms, one can do it atop the atmosphere. I have developed a mathematical formula for predicting air mass movements up to one month in advance. Under certain conditions, six months. No official weather service can do that, sir."

"Would it be impolite to ask why you bring this valuable scientific data to me, and perhaps through me to the Chinese, when your own government would reward you handsomely for it?"

Time for a fastball right down the middle.

"They think I'm nuts, Sir Edmund."

"Ah."

"Do you?"

"Think you're barmy? No, no. Let me assure you, I have seen too much of this world and its treatment of genius to miss your point. I knew Einstein, you know."

"Einstein? Really?"

"Him and others. Other neglected geniuses. Wilde? Baudelaire, if you can believe it. Aubrey Beardsley." He must have seen that his literary brag list was losing Pa, who didn't have much nonscientific culture beyond Joseph Jenks and His Weather Machine.

"Perhaps most significantly, I have known dozens of the stars of Chinese science. Have you ever seen acupuncture demonstrated, Commander?"

I had, in an open stall in the Ch'ien Men, and it had scared the daylights out of me.

"I don't believe so, Sir Edmund."

"Marvelous technique for the relief of pain. The doctor inserts dozens of needles into the flesh. I was myself cured of arthritis by acupuncture." He flexed his hands to show how cured. "I know a fellow who showed the doctors at St. Michael's Hospital, in the French legation, that the rotten curd of the soya bean will clear an infection. You should have seen the dear nuns roll up their eyes and scurry."

Pa was getting itchy listening to someone else's spiel.

"Ah, but to return to your formula. Would you put it into my hands so that I might study it, along with the observational data on which it is based? Have no fear, I hold two degrees in mathematics and physics from the Sorbonne."

Would he? Pa almost tore his pocket digging out the notebook and pressing it into the hands of Backhouse.

There was, it turned out, just one other thing. If we had wondered ever so slightly before why Sir Edmund had invited us in after all these years of hinting around for an invitation, we soon knew the answer.

Like Pa, Sir Edmund was convinced—"absolutely unimpeachable sources, you understand"—that the Japanese were about to attack Peking. In defense of both of them, so woefully wrong about so much else, that attack did come just a few months later, across the Marco Polo Bridge south of the city. That catastrophe being imminent, the Hermit of Peking believed that his life's work, in manuscript and folio all around him, and also his life, which he waved away carelessly, were in danger.

He wanted to know, in so many words, if there was any chance the American Embassy would offer him their hospitality if the Japanese attack came.

Pa was flabbergasted. "But, Sir Edmund, surely you'd prefer to go to the British Embassy, where they'd receive you with open arms."

How could he have known that already there was a waiting list of British officials who coveted tickets to the old bugger's hanging?

Sir Edmund did his version of the crestfallen martyr. "I'm very much afraid, Commander, that they think I'm, ah, nuts."

That locked it.

"But let us just say for now, Commander, that I am taking out an assurance policy. Do you? Think they would?"

Pa spoke for all of us. "I can guarantee it. You and your books and papers would be welcome there and safe."

"Careful. The papers are rather voluminous. My Chinese dictionary alone—well, twenty years' work. And the court diaries ... Between us, Commander, I'm thinking now of leaving the entire corpus to the Vatican Library. You are a Catholic, Commander, are you not?"

"Why, yes, sir."

"Then you will see my point. The Bodleian—at Oxford?—has been such a disappointment with their clumsy handling of my earlier gifts." The saintly looking old fake put a long-nailed finger to his lips. "Shh, let's keep it between us Catholics for now, eh. I am, God forgive me, a rather late convert to the Faith. Actually, *Pio Nono* said to me when I was quite a small child," —Pius the Ninth?—" 'Edmund, God wants you in the true fold.' " He sketched his boyhood meeting with the Pope, and threw in later conversations with Huysmans, Beardsley, and Cardinal Newman—*cor ad cor loquitor*, as we used to say in Lakewood, New Jersey: "heart speaketh unto heart"—who all begged him to come over to Rome. He was to write all that in his scurrilous autobiography later. And I thought Pa was an eccentric!

The two of them started in on the gifts and services of the seventeenth-century Jesuits to China in science and religion, not to mention diplomacy.

"Did you know, child," the old scholar said to me in Chinese

105

suddenly, "that the only existing treaty establishing a lawful border between China and Russia is written in Latin? Eh?"

I tried not to look like a kid on the street yelling vulgar remarks, and answered in the same language. "No sir. That's very interesting, sir."

"Yes, it is. That's because Jesuit priests wrote it. Diplomats. Oh, I should think so."

I was mesmerized by this single sentence he addressed to me all that afternoon. What must it be like to have the full force of that personality turned on you?

All the way home Pa chortled and smacked his fist into his palm and told the world what a great man Sir Edmund was and planned his own apotheosis as Scientific Advisor when the Manchus marched back into power, a modern-day unfrocked Jesuit bringing True Meteorological Science to the numskull heathen.

Every time he smacked his palm, though, our rickshaw boy would look back fearfully and try to run faster.

"Go slower, idiot," I yelled at him in street dialect, but it only seemed to make him more panicked. The trip almost killed him. I slipped him an extra penny at the end. He was either ecstatic or having a heart attack.

Francis appeared at my door the next day, unexpected and beaming with pleasure at his own ingenuity.

"Here I am. Illegally, I might add. If my government knew that I am here, they would throw a classical Chinese fit. Your government, too, yes. May I come in, please, Neil?"

I could scarcely shut the door in his face. "How did you get here if neither England nor China wants you to leave London?"

He raised his hands to fend off my questions. "I am, of course, with my fast friends, the Middle Eastern friends of the People's Republic, conferring on how to exchange oil for technology. Very secret, locked rooms and all that. We will probably be locked in that perishing room all day." He clapped his hands and rushed over to my sea view.

"Oh, how very beautiful. Oh, you lucky Neil, having this lovely beach just outside your digs." He wagged his head from side to side in admiration. "I must smoke. You don't

106

like it, I know, but you must forgive me and let me puff away my lungs." He held the cigarette in the tips of his fingers and puffed like a wicked fat little boy. "Am I interrupting your work on the book about the priest who was a poet?"

"As a matter of fact, yes. At least, I was getting very little done, but it now appears I won't get anything done." I sat in my one easy chair and watched him. He had turned into quite a compulsive performer.

"I said that I would not reveal how I got here, but it is so delicious that I must tell you. Yes, today I am with the Japanese bus of tourists. The tour guide is a kind of cousin of mine, you see. The Japanese think I am a sociologist, studying their habits abroad. I have a big clipboard in the bus. And ballpoint pens in three colors. Very sociological, eh? I speak better Japanese than most of them, so we chatter happily away about how they like the toilet paper and if Brussels sprouts are delicious and so on. Now they are off to see the childhood home of Sir Walter Raleigh in East Budleigh, you know."

"What is it today, Francis?"

"Ah, do you mean what load of cock and bull do I have for you today?" He giggled and sat into my sofa, leaving his feet an inch from the floor. He grimaced helplessly and slipped off his loafers and tucked his feet under him. "None, I assure you. But I do want to tell you about a project of which I am the Director in Peking, because among other things, we will honor the memory of your father, the Commander, there."

"I'm going to need some coffee. You?"

"Please."

I went into my cubicle kitchen and kept listening to him through the pass-through into the living room. In the tidy quarters of my apartment he was only ten feet away.

"It is an historical reconstruction project. You would not know the old Legation Quarter now, Neil. New construction everywhere. And we are building a Center for Western Heroes of the People. Yes, good foreigners, you know, who contributed to Chinese modernization. From Marco Polo—

107

who was actually the governor of a whole Chinese province the size of England for seventeen years—and the great Father Ricci and his Jesuit comrades, who really brought us all our western science and taught us western diplomacy, down to such contemporary great men as Edmund Backhouse and the Commander."

I poured the water from my saucepan on top of the powdered coffee. "Sugar? Milk?"

"Yes, please, both. White coffee, as we say."

"Are you asking my permission to put up a plaque with Pa's name on it?"

"Oh, much more than a plaque, Neil. Thank you. Ah, delicious. Perhaps a small room, with models of his early instruments, photographs—rather like the baseball Hall of Fame, you know. Continuous filmstrips telling the story in four languages for visitors. The whole ball of wax." He grinned over his cup. "That is a new expression I acquired from a young lady in the Hilton Hotel yesterday. A saucy little bird who did not mind having sex with this terrible foreign fat man for fifty quid."

"Knock it off, Francis, whatever all that nonsense is about. You don't need my permission to put a Commander Kelly room in your hall of good foreigners."

"Neil, Neil, why are you so hostile? This is simply a courtesy. And who knows? If you would like to come to the dedication of my Center when it opens in 1985, the People's Republic of China would welcome you as the son of one of our greatest heroes."

"Kelly and Backhouse. Some heroes. Why don't you call it the Frauds' Wing? They were both con men, deluded by their own dreams, Francis, and I'm beginning to think your dreams might have you by the throat, too, my old chum."

"Ah, yes. You have read the estimable Trevor-Roper's bad book about Sir Edmund, haven't you? And you took it in hook, line, and sinker, in the American phrase, eh?"

He lit a new cigarette from the old one. "I learned much of my American idiom from the Commander, and I suppose it is somewhat out of date."

I hated his filthy cigarette smoke. I went to the window and pushed it open. The surf was noisy in the wind and the breeze was westerly now, in from the Atlantic. I stayed near the window to get the fresh air.

"Let me tell you about Sir Edmund, Neil. After all, your Professor Trevor-Roper is not really a scholar of Chinese language or history at all, is he? The Regius Professor of History at Oxford, yes, but he has written what? A book on the English religious wars of the seventeenth century? A book about Hitler? Yet he thinks he has solved the intricate problem of the Hermit of Peking.

"I have been up to Oxford, you know, to which Sir Edmund contributed so magnificently in Chinese manuscripts and books. Go see, if you doubt it. There is a plaque in the Bodleian Library, inscribed with his name, thanking him for his benefactions. And now they say, 'Oh well, we were wrong about that. The old gentlemen went native, y'know, and got barmy as a coot in China before he died. Actually forged all those so-called documents.'" Francis did a magnificent music-hall upper crust English accent, with gestures. He really should have been an actor.

"So I went up to their Bodleian Library, and I sat down at this lovely old oak table which they had pilfered from some monastery they burnt down years ago, and I said to their Board of Governors this: 'Very well, gentlemen,' I said, 'we believe that Backhouse was a great man and an honest man. You think him a great fraud who faked these remarkable gifts to your deservedly world-famous library. So, give them back to us. They are only fakes,' I said, 'so why not simply get rid of them?'

"Oh, they have some monetary value, of course, Neil, but I offered them that—whatever they had paid Sir Edmund for them, plus interest for their storage all these years."

He jumped to his feet and paced back and forth excitedly.

"Fragments of the original *Yung-lo* Encyclopedia, Neil. Absolutely priceless. The *Ku Chin T'u Shu Chi Ch'eng* of the *Yung-ch'eng* Emperor! That is one thousand, six hundred, and twenty volumes alone, Neil, a wonder of the world. The Chinese invented the encyclopedia, you know. Backhouse gave them autographs of the Dowager Empress Tzu-hsi, spectacular calligraphy by K'ang-hsi, the contemporary of Louis XIV, and ruler of fifty times as great an empire. The family sayings of Confucius are there. Neil, would you believe that? In the Bodley. The *Tso Commentary* edition of the *Spring and Autumn Annals*. It is as though we were talking about original documents of Plato's Academy, or of St. John's manuscript of the First Gospel." He collapsed on the sofa exhausted from his passion.

"Whew. I think I will give myself a heart attack some day if I am not prudent. Do you see the problem, Neil? They have these things—things, I say—these treasures from Sir Edmund, and they say, oh, but they are just rubbish. But when I say to them, very well, gentlemen, sell me your rubbish for this many hundred thousand pounds sterling, they say, oh, we cannot do that, Mr. Li. Oh, not on your life, sir. You explain that to me, Neil."

"I can't explain it, and you know it. I'm not a Chinese scholar."

He shrugged eloquently. He was, of course, in more ways than one.

"But I have read the Trevor-Roper book, Francis, and it's convincing, absolutely. Look, just for example. Sir Edmund relied on the so-called Li Lien-ying memoirs for a lot of the detail in his Manchu court history, right?"

"Correct. Absolutely."

"But those memoirs don't exist and never did. Old Li Lien-ying did, but not his memoirs. Another invention of the fertile brain of Sir Edmund."

"Tell me what you know about Li Lien-ying, Neil. Apart from what you have read in Trevor-Roper's scurrilous book."

"Zero."

"Yes. A good, brief American summary. Zero. Well, I know more than zero. Please notice that we have the same family name, Li."

"Which is the Chinese equivalent of Smith."

"True. But there are Smiths, and some of them are related to others." He lit another of his poisonous cigarettes and waved the match out in the smoke. "Li Lien-ying was a Peking cobbler as a young man. Immensely ambitious. Even for a cousin of mine. The family say he was very tall, had one of your prominent western noses. Who knows why? In any case, whether he had a touch of European blood and brains or not, he was different from the other cobblers of Peking. He eventually became the chief eunuch of the Manchu court. Do you know how one does that?"

"Well, apart from the obvious, no."

He laughed. "You know the old joke? A little boy asked an old bald man one day, 'What is a eunuch?' and the old man said, 'A eunuch is a balled man.' And the little boy said, 'Are you a eunuch? And the old man said, 'No, sonny, I am two balled.' Ah, I love English puns." He choked giggling and continued. "But I digress. First of all, Li Lien-ying castrated himself. Zip. Just like that. And then he presented himself to the palace as a leather worker. And he was, a very good one. And by sheer meanness and brilliance he outfoxed his rivals and became eventually the Chief Eunuch. One might as well say the Prime Minister, because it was the functional equivalent of that. Remember that he who controls the royal harem decides which child is legitimate—controls, in fact, the line of succession to the throne. He became immensely wealthy. And he kept both the daily accounts and a personal diary for more than thirty years in the court of that wicked old woman, the Dowager Empress, last of the Manchus. She was our Nero, you know, murderer of her brothers and sisters, poisoner of several lovers, insatiable nymphomaniac, an incredible organizational genius— perhaps Nero and Catherine the Great rolled into one."

"Do you actually believe that Backhouse was her lover, as he claimed in his diary?"

"There is no question of it. They were both geniuses, and I think they needed each other's company. It is, as you Americans like to say, very lonely at the top, Neil. One needs a friend, even if just one, believe me."

He was a spellbinder; I almost believed him.

111

"But the so-called memoirs of your chief eunuch have never been found. They presumably don't exist."

"There are two possible answers to that, Neil. The first is that the original manuscripts of the Gospels have never been found. Are they therefore all forgeries? A better answer is, oh yes, I have *seen* them." He leaned toward me to touch my chest with his finger as he said it.

"They were in the house at number 19 Shih-Fuma Street, a house you visited with your father, the Commander, once, Neil. Trevor-Roper says they were 'supposed' to have been burned by the Japanese in 1939. Well, they were not. When Sir Edmund was in his terminal illness, he was moved at his request to St. Michael's Hospital, in the French section of the Legation, after having been in residence in the old Austrian Legation, which you recall, was a sort of neutral house for all foreigners after 1920. He tried to move in with the Americans and with the British and God knows with whom else, but no one would have him. No room at the inn, so to speak.

"When he was hospitalized, boxes and boxes of his papers—we are speaking of perhaps two or three hundred volumes—were stored in the basement of St. Michael's. I have them now." He bowed modestly. "They will, of course, be enshrined in the appropriate wing of the new Center when it opens in 1985. They include the Li Lien-ying diary, my friend."

"Did you tell them that at the Bodleian when you were there?"

"Think. Why should I? It would authenticate their so-called fake collection. As it is, there is still some hope, if they continue to believe they hold only fakes, that they will see the good sense of selling them back to the poor gullible Chinese for a few hundred thousand pounds. Oxford is a very poor university by your standards, Neil. I imagine Harvard could buy all of Oxford with their endowment and have enough left over to buy Cambridge."

"What's the point of telling me all this, Francis?"

"The point is what is not in the papers of Sir Edmund

Backhouse, Neil. I was sure that your father's final note-books would be there. They were not. Your father, the Commander, gave Sir Edmund the formula, didn't he?"

"Oh, for Pete's sake, Francis."

"He did have a formula, you know, Neil. I'm sure of it. You told me yourself that he did, the day after you had visited 19 Shih-Fuma Street in 1937. You told me, Neil."

"I told you because I thought it was a pathetic joke. Two old men swapping secrets in the Tartar City. One afraid people would find out he was a Catholic convert and one afraid people would *not* find out he had discovered the secret of atmospheric magic, infallible weather forecast-ing."

"I'll tell you something, Neil, flat out. I would swap the whole Bodleian collection, and the Li Lien-ying diary too, and all the gorgeous calligraphy of the K'ang-hsi Emperor for that formula. That's how much I believe in it."

We were shouting now, the two of us with our necks jut-ting out like fighting cocks, waving and raving.

"He couldn't even predict the weather for the next day most of the time, did you realize that? My mother used to smile at me when he would plan a picnic or an outing, because it was as likely to rain as not. We got caught in a terrible dust storm out north of the city once on a ride to go kite flying. No one else was out to fly kites that day, but Pa said not to worry, they were all probably at some religious festival chasing away devils. They simply had enough sense to know there was a dust storm coming, Francis. But not the infallible Commander. We were lost for four damn hours, and almost choked to death before we found a trail back south."

"Behavior typical of genius, Neil. The large picture is so clear that they do not always see the small one. Think of Einstein, who always forgot dinner invitations, often did not remember how to get home from class."

"Einstein my foot."

"Einstein. What if he had stayed in Germany? Another poor Jew with his ribs sticking out, hanging on the barbed

113

wire at Dachau when the American troops came in? And if he had said to them, 'Please, young men, I have in my brain a formula that will transform the way we think about the universe, will perhaps give us a new, infinitely renewable source of immense energy,' what do you think your GI's would have said? 'Sure, old man. Just take it easy and we'll get you some hot food and a bath.' 'Oh,' Einstein says, 'but you don't understand. E equals mc squared.' 'That's swell, old man,' the GI in charge of delousing him says, 'now just stand over there, please, and we'll get these goddam bugs off you.' Eh? Couldn't it have been like that? It was just a formula in a funny old man's head, wasn't it? It was the formula for the future history of mankind, Neil!"

"Francis, if you can believe my father had anything anywhere near that, you will believe anything."

"Are you saying that you think the Commander lied?" He looked genuinely shocked.

"Of course. He lied all the time. He boasted, he imagined, he theorized, he hypothesized, and he ended by believing all of it himself. But very, very little of it was true. My father was a crank, Francis."

He sat back and lit a cigarette and shook out the match with an amused look, as though he had received a satisfactory answer to a very tricky question.

"You must say that, of course. Your government would scarcely permit otherwise, eh?"

"I forgot. You think I'm a spy. God knows for whom. You're a bit of a crank yourself, do you know that, old boy? Or as we Americans like to say, chum, you're getting to be an awful pain in the ass, Francis."

"I was told a funny thing the other day, Neil."

"Well, I could use a laugh. This book I'm not writing has begun to sit on my chest at night smiling at me like a goddam Cheshire cat. Plenty of grin, but no substance. Cheer me up."

"When you flew from Boston to London this past fortnight? What an excellent English word, I do think perhaps it is my favorite English word. Fortnight. Yes. Well, in any

114

case, your ticket was bought and paid for by whom? Have you forgotten?"

"By a woman you never even heard of. She was returning a favor."

"Never heard of? Come on, Neil. This is your old chum Francis. Never heard of Mary Dowd of the CIA?" He squinted through his cigarette smoke and grinned at me. It was another kind of Cheshire-cat grin, lewd and knowing.

"It would be difficult to explain, but if you really want to know the facts, I'll tell you."

He clapped his hands. "I love the facts. Do."

"Mary Dowd was assigned to a case of murder and international industrial espionage in the United States. I got involved in that case only because, and only to the extent that, some friends of mine were the victims. Mary Dowd and I began by disliking each other intensely, and at the end of it we had what I suppose we could call a grudging mutual respect. The ticket was her way—perhaps her boss's way—of apologizing for the hassle that delayed my vacation so long."

"Ah. Good. Like a dozen roses after a lovers' quarrel."

"Christ."

"So. You freely admit that during this past year you were working with CIA agents—and perhaps FBI agents, too?—on a major international criminal conspiracy, and you still want me to accept you as a virgin? Come off it, Neil, as you Yankees say."

"Forget it. Your paranoia or mystical insight or whatever it is is showing again."

"You and Gus were both in the secret services of your respective countries during the war. You, I gather, were a principal agent for the American navy in intercepting and decoding Japanese secret weather broadcasts. Very nice. And now you two old friends are reunited again. For what purpose, I ask myself over and over? Why should these two old chums just happen to be getting together now? And you know, Neil, I think I have the answer."

"Any answer you get to that question won't be worth

much, Francis, so stick it in your ear. Gus and I met by chance and I am living in his house by chance."

"So many chances. Such great odds against all these coincidences happening, yet they happen. I think it is either a miracle or a careful plan, Neil, my old friend. And although I am still a Christian down deep, I have never really believed in miracles. Q.E.D." He shrugged helplessly. "I am at the mercy of logic. Something is up, yes, eh?"

I felt myself moved by one of the most urgent and powerful motives a man can feel. I wanted to punch this fat little grinning son of a bitch right in the nose. And I think he knew it. And I think he was not afraid of it. If he had set out to goad me to fury, he had succeeded.

I shouted at him for five minutes without stopping. I insulted him and I said that I was ashamed to know him. That he had taken our old friendship and made it into some kind of lever for playing his insane games. That I wanted none of it, and that if he didn't stop it I was going to kick his fat Chinese ass right out the door.

"Let me tell you what the Russians are doing, Neil. Just for two minutes, and then if you want to kick this poor old pain-in-the-Chinese-ass out your door, I will gladly bend over for you."

"Goddam it, Francis, I don't want to hear about the Russians or the starving peasantry of the Middle Kingdom or Alice in Wonderland or any of it," I shouted at him.

I should have saved my voice. He had been shouted at by experts. As soon as I had stopped yelling he began again.

"For five years in the 1970s, Neil, Japan had its worst snows in history. China, a land not unfamiliar with drought on a scale Americans cannot imagine, had enormous droughts. Millions dead. Europe had weather unrecorded since the eighteenth century. England nearly dried up. England! Five summers in a row. As a matter of fact, a literary historian pointed out that entries in a literary diary he was editing, a diary written in 1776, had entries of weather observations nearly identical with those in England that year." He paused and mused over what he was saying.

"As though someone was recreating it, he said. Russia, in those years except the last, Neil, had record wheat crops, good rain, a good balance of rain, and warm growing weather. In the last year Russia too was smashed by terrible weather, especially in winter. Some scientists think that it was only then that the experiment was called off, that something had gone awry."

"Are you saying that for five years the Russians were changing the weather around the world? Doing the kind of thing my poor nutty father wanted to do by blowing steam heat up the Great Wall of China?"

"I am saying that it is within the realm of possibility. That with what we did know of Russian advances in meteorological sciences, it is even a probability. They haven't got the final methodology yet, but perhaps if they had just one more piece in the puzzle . . ."

"Francis, go home. I know what it is now. You are simply a crank. Like my poor deluded father. You are a bigger crank than he ever was, and I suppose you are in a position to make more waves—no pun intended—but you are just another crank. I grew up with one, Francis. It's like growing up with a drunk; you never want to repeat the experience. Go home." I put my face in my hands and groaned. I felt like weeping with rage and frustration. Little Francis Li had grown up to be the Commander's perfect disciple, a convinced fanatic, and he apparently thought I had the goddam key to his insane dream of glory.

"Actually, Neil, the day is rapidly approaching when almost any describable weather phenomena can be generated experimentally on a large scale. Think of that. Far cheaper than sending an army to attack an enemy. Send a single hurricane, for example, releasing more energy than a nuclear warhead." He walked over to my window and looked out over the Channel.

"There is the English Channel, is it not? Here you are, at, what? fifty-odd degrees of latitude north—like the middle of Alaska, eh: Fifty-four forty or fight. Seward's icebox. But it is not an icebox here, is it? Down the coast there twenty

117

miles at Torquay you can see the famous palm trees growing. Why? You know why, because the Gulf Stream is out there. The same river of warm water that keeps all Norway's ports ice-free all winter. Did you know, Neil, that Benjamin Franklin, that great genius who liked to fly kites and so on, proposed to the American Continental Congress during your Revolutionary War that they appropriate money to study the feasibility of diverting the Gulf Stream away from England, so that these islands would become ice-locked, like Russia? It is true."

I knew. I had read it incredulously in college. It had reminded me of Pa.

"It was a magnificent idea for the eighteenth century, but a trifle premature. Congress thought he was insane, of course."

I was saying nothing. Francis seemed unstoppable unless I really wanted to get violent. I wanted to let him get it all out of his system.

"Your country has signed an international treaty, you know, Neil—is it possible that you do not know?—in which all the parties pledge themselves not to engage in weather modification experiments for strategic military or commercial purposes."

"Since you think I'm some kind of high-level spy, you aren't going to believe me when I tell you I didn't know that, but I didn't."

"Well, let us say that most Americans probably don't. That treaty established the Global Atmospheric Research Program, GARP, which is an international study of weather management—management, mind you, and forecasting. Now, that takes care of the problem, does it not? We all know that the Russians, for example, would never dream of contravening an international treaty. Another Li's Law for you. I call that asinine view of reality The World According to GARP. Eh?"

"Well, Francis, someone must be taking the problem seriously, if we have bothered to negotiate a treaty concerning the management and forecasting of weather. If anything, I find that reassuring."

118

"Don't be too reassured, Neil. Your father, the Commander, used to complain to me that the U.S. Weather Bureau spent just two cents per citizen on scientific meteorology. If he were alive now he would see that they are not doing much better. They say, your Weather Bureau, that it is impossible to predict the weather more than five days ahead. What is the saying at West Point? 'The generals are always preparing for the last war'? What nonsense that five-day limit is, Neil. You have the world's greatest weather scientists at Cal Tech, and they are now predicting the weather accurately months ahead of time. But even they lack the final key. Do you know what I think that key is, Neil, my old friend?"

Here it was at last. Reduced to its simples, he thought Pa had found the golden key.

"Hasn't it occurred to you, Neil, that the Russians are aware that you have that key in your possession, and that they are making an effort to take it away from you?"

"Oh, for Christ sake, Francis. Is that what you've made out of that silly story I told you and Gus about my house being robbed and the cottage thing here?"

He turned dramatically away from the window and looked sadly at me and shrugged. Academy Award stuff. He dropped his pudgy hands halfway through a new gesture and walked to the door like a beaten man.

"I have been trying to tell you that you are in danger, Neil. That my intelligence people say you are in extreme danger. Well, I have tried. Even to say that much is a grave crime for me, an official of the Chinese People's government. All very top secret, you know. Please appreciate at least that much I have tried to do for you. If you were to report this conversation to my embassy, I would get a far worse punishment than merely carrying shit for the next many years. Do be careful, my old chum."

"Wild horses and all that stuff, Francis."

"Yes, yes. Wild horses. I hope so sincerely." He stopped on his way out the door and pointed to the two Kyoto bottles on my mantle. "Didn't you have those two pretty bottles in your parents' house in Peking when we were children?"

"You have a good memory; yes, they are the same two."

"How do you say it? They have been bugging me. I am glad that you take such care of your family heirlooms. Filial piety is not a Chinese monopoly, I suppose."

After he left I stood for a long time myself staring out at the sea. The surf was far higher now, and there were white-caps to the horizon. The waves crashed terrifically on themselves and churned the beach to red foam in the Devon mud, like a tide of dark blood. It was going to rain hard soon. The noise of the ocean was deafening.

14

THE MURDER OF the child, and of Libby and her brother Robert, turned my resentment and muddle about Francis and the notebooks to a white hot, burning rage.

I learned about it only on Monday morning. I had been working at my table, writing an analysis of the word "death" in Donne's sermons. "Every man's death diminishes me, because I am involved in mankind." The assertion is important, with its insistence on the single death of each person. Death as an abstraction means nothing, and Donne knew that, just as he knew that Life in some sense abstracted from someone living it has only conceptual, not existential reality. But if the death of all means nothing, the death of any one means everything, because in some way it is my own. I am involved in it by both seeming in some way to suffer it and to cause it.

I grumbled immoderately when the doorbell rang and I could hear the feet on the stairs, ascending. If it was Francis again I was prepared to blow my top.

It was Constable Howe, though, and behind him two other men, pretty obviously policemen.

"It's me, again, Professor. I wonder if we could come in for a bit, sir."

I sighed for my ebbing inspiration about Donne and death and opened the door wider to let them into my living room, which now seemed much smaller.

Howe introduced each of his followers as they came in. The first was Detective Inspector Nicholas Hawley. The other was Detective Sergeant John Pride. Hawley was lean and quick, with a foxy face. Pride was a slugger, a wide, bearish man with the neck and jaw of a defensive lineman.

Hawley took over the moment and asked Constable Howe if he would perhaps get back to the station now and stay near the phone until they returned, but bring up any messages from someone named More—his boss, I supposed.

Then the horror began.

Hawley told me crisply and quietly what had happened, so far as they had been able to piece it together.

The body of the woman Libby had been found first, in the kitchen of Gus's house, by Gus and Sue when they returned about half past noon from church services. She had been stabbed with a kitchen knife.

Her brother Robert had also been stabbed, twice, but had somehow crawled out of the house and across the yard to the gill, leaving a trail of blood as he went. He had been found lying face down in the stream, the knife still in his back, arms outstretched. Just beyond his reach, in the water, tangled in the overgrowth on the edge, the infant's body was found, dead from either a crushed skull or drowning, they didn't know yet, lying partially in, partially out of a red toy boat.

". . . Sort of a toy dory, you know, a pretty thing."

Hawley was watching my reaction, and made a quick gesture to his sergeant when I looked as though I was going to faint. I know I reeled for a moment. I could feel the color and the warmth drain from me, as though the life was flooding out of me into the floor. Then the reaction came in its opposite form, and a scream of rage and horror was in my throat choking me to be let out. I stumbled into the kitchen on Pride's arm and vomited my scream and my tears and my guts into the sink.

The two men waited patiently while I toweled the sweat and mess from myself and washed my face off in cold water. Hawley turned his back and looked out over the sea.

We all sat down in the living room, and after I had stared into my hands for a minute or an hour, Inspector Hawley began again.

I asked him about Gus and Sue.

"The mother's in a state of shock, you understand. Their family doctor put her in hospital under sedation right off. Mr. Van Duren went down there with her, but just to stay by. He'll be all right. You understand."

The professional judgment. Hawley had seen more than a few bereft, grief-maddened parents in his thirty years a cop. Had seen them recover slowly and in a pain of bewilderment at what had happened in their lives, to their lives, back to something that would pass for normalcy. Able to function and work and go on with it apparently, but dead themselves somewhere inside because a piece of them had been killed outside their bodies.

Constable Howe had told them apologetically of the "coincidence" I had told him about, my house in Oldhampton being burgled and then the cottage I had hired in Ottery St. Mary getting vandalized in what looked like an unsuccessful burglary attempt.

Hawley raised his right eyebrow, which caused his left eye to droop. It was his way of framing a question; I was to become very familiar with the gesture.

"So there we are, Professor Kelly. What on earth do you make of it, if you wouldn't mind saying."

I started to talk before I realized that my voice wouldn't work properly, and had to clear my throat, which burned from the retching, and start again.

"My God."

"Yes. It's a terrible crime. As bad as I've ever seen, when you think of it. The child, and then the retarded boy, trying, I suppose, to go after them, to save the baby, perhaps. Mr. Van Duren says he was devoted to the baby. He loved to hold him, he said."

"Sweet God in heaven."

"Would you mind if Sergeant Pride made us all some tea or coffee? Whatever you have in the kitchen will do." He didn't wait for my delayed-action nod, but jerked his head toward the kitchen to Pride.

"Yes, sure. There's both there in the cabinet next to the stove. The cooker."

He bore on relentlessly, making me hear it, so that I could absorb it and hold it in focus somehow and deal with it as what it was, the reality we faced.

"What we can't figure is what they were after. Or why they should break into the house in broad daylight and

123

then, apparently unprepared to do any bodily harm, grab up the nearest weapon in the kitchen and start killing anyone there."

"Why did they take the baby? I mean, if he was down in the stream . . . ?"

"Yes. It doesn't make sense, does it. A kidnapping? Spur of the moment? Didn't find what they were really after, so grabbed up the child? Possible, I suppose."

I shook my head, as much to clear it as to indicate to Hawley that I disagreed with his thinking. Did I? My mind refused to perform its regular job. I couldn't think logically. I felt as though I had been run over. My ears were ringing, and I couldn't tell if it was the surge of the sea outside or my own pulse beating.

I could see Sergeant Pride through the pass-through, cleaning up my sink with a housewife's finicky care, washing down the mess I had made. He washed his hands with my green dishwashing liquid and rinsed and dried them before he poured out three cups of boiling water over teabags and set them on a tray with the sugar and the little carton of milk from my refrigerator and brought it all in neatly and set it on the table.

We each took a cup and sipped it in silence.

"I'm sorry about the mess," I said to the sergeant with a helpless gesture.

"Nothing at all, sir. We clean up a lot of messes. Part of the job."

The routine of it had a calming effect. It seemed they had been there for hours, although it could not have been more than twenty minutes since they had introduced themselves.

"If nothing occurs to you now, Professor Kelly, I can understand that. But you understand we'll be in and out several times more, and be asking you to come down to the station and, I'm afraid, too, over to the Van Duren house, before this is done."

I nodded dumbly. "Look, call me Neil, please. If we can be a little informal, it might help."

Neither of them said anything. Perhaps it was against the rules. In any case, it would, I thought. Help us communicate across the professional calm in them and the emotional wreckage in me.

Hawley apparently decided that our having met and my learning about the murders was enough to take from this session. He gulped the rest of his tea and gestured minutely to his sergeant, who finished his own in one swallow and moved toward the door.

"We'll go back to our other business now, sir," Hawley said.

"I'm sorry we had to tell you this bad news, sir," Pride said in his controlled boom of a voice. His accent was northern.

"You know where the police station is, if you want to talk to me or to Sergeant Pride about anything at all?"

"Yes, I know." It was the front room of a small house called Seawalk, half a dozen doors up from mine.

"There's an emergency phone there in the glass box beside the door if no one's on duty. I see you have no phone here. Just use the emergency if you need to, or call this number." He jotted an Exmouth number on a card and gave it to me. "We must set up an inquiry room there, you see, to collect and sort out the facts."

"We'll have the lads done this, sir," Pride said in his quiet rumble. Hawley didn't seem to mind his sergeant having his say. They seemed to like each other.

15

I HAD WANTED to see Gus on Tuesday, the day after I learned about the murders, but he would see no one. He was at the hospital, sitting at Sue's bedside, waiting for her to speak to him or to cry or to give any sign that she hadn't died, too, along with their son.

I tried to talk to a doctor or to one of the nurses, but that was impossible, too. The newspapers and the police between them had forced the hospital staff to barricade themselves behind a wall of silence and rules, and no one was getting any more information than was being issued in daily bulletins down at the front desk.

The newspapers ate it up, of course, the sensation of the triple murder, the sentimental exploitation turning the tragedy to soap opera, to cheap melodrama with lurid headlines and improbable speculations about Mad Killers Loose in Devon and Butcher's Holiday in Seaside Resort. British newspapers put the yellowest of American tabloids in the shade when they start on any story, and this was their story of the decade.

My morning walk through the village center for a cup of coffee and scones at the cafe and a paper at the newsagent's became a kind of gauntlet. Apparently, as I had expected, everyone knew that the Yank who had moved in down on the shore just a few weeks ago had been visited by the police several times. I was considering not going into the stores at all, and stopped dropping by the Raleigh's Cask for an evening pint until Detective Inspector Hawley made it right by simply suggesting we take a pint together while we talked. He knew what was up, and he knew the cure for it. Helping the police with their inquiries can mean you're under suspicion, but if you and the chief cop on the case are drinking together in the evening, just maybe you're actually helping the police with their inquiries.

Detective Inspector Nicholas Hawley of the Devon and Cornwall Constabulary told me to call him Nick.

"Or Hooker."

I raised an eyebrow, and suddenly realized I was unconsciously imitating him.

"Ask me why. Everybody else does."

"All right. Why do they call you Hooker?"

"Started when I was a lad. Hell of a football player, I was. Had a savage kick, crooked like. I'd run right at my man and kick the ball and it would zoom off to the left at a terrific angle. I couldn't help it any more than a golfer can help hooking his swing sometimes. Fooled the boys I played with, mostly. Gave me the idea I'd play for Manchester United or Arsenal before I was twenty." He grunted and laughed shortly.

"But the professionals simply overplayed you to that side."

"You've got it in one. Know football?"

"Not a thing beyond the rudiments. But I played a little baseball when I was young. Dead pull hitter."

He hmphed. "Hooker, you mean."

"Hooker, right. The first time we played a team they'd play me straight away, or maybe shade me to my right, since I'm not very big. Then I'd pull two or three down the third base line for hits. After that they'd overplay me to the left field line, and my batting average would drop like a stone. Never could learn to hit to right."

"Two of a kind then."

We were sitting in the Raleigh's Cask saloon bar, having a pint apiece, the day after Hawley and Sergeant Pride had first come to my door with the terrible news of the multiple tragedy at the Van Durens'.

When he and Pride had left me that morning, I had stood for a long time staring out over the sea. The sky had become silver with overcast, and the sea was silver. After a while a long, bright column of yellow light had poured through a hole in the overcast and lit the sea green for a few minutes. Then it clouded over again and started a thin drizzle.

The morning after Hooker and I had got a little tight together in front of one and all at the Cask, the news reporters were on to me like flies on honey. Well, I had learned how to deal with reporters back in Oldhampton, when another friend of mine had been murdered, and I shut them out without a word of conversation. One result was a story in the *Southwest News* under the headline "Top Yank Crimesolver Called In By Cops", to the effect that I was being heavily relied on by the police to solve the whole case for them. I learned that I was a well-known American criminologist by avocation, and that I had solved countless baffling cases, some said by psychic powers, for the FBI.

The local police use one technique that I thought had gone out seventy-five years ago, the appeal poster.

Two days after the murders, great twelve-by-eighteen-inch yellow paper posters appeared in every shop and on every public wall.

Under the escutcheon of the Devon and Cornwall police, *In Auxilium Omnium*, the word MURDER was painted in red strokes three inches high. Beneath it was the word APPEAL.

On Sunday 24th May 1981
Elizabeth Grandisson, Robert Grandisson and Richard Van Duren were murdered at the home of Austin and Susan Van Duren, a detached house in Lower Mill Lane, Raleigh's Gill.

Were you in this area between 8 am and 1 pm on that day?

Did you see anything suspicious, or anyone acting suspiciously?

Has a stranger called at your home?

If you have any information, however insignificant it might seem, contact the police.

'PHONE: EXMOUTH 4651

All in heavy black marker, staring at me from every side.

128

I tried to remember the faces of Libby Grandisson and her poor brother. Hers was easier, because she had been so carven, so statuesque in the precision and classical curve of her lips and eyes and her short, perfectly straight nose. Robert I could remember only as one remembers the severely retarded, a face blurred by the absence of even low normal intelligence, rather doggish and gentle and droopy-eyed.

I remembered him being given little Richard to hold for the picture-taking outside the church. He had held the tiny bundle ecstatically, tenderly, beaming with pride at the camera; but at the exact moment of the picture lowering his head to kiss the baby's cheek, an irresistible impulse of love. Libby had groaned and explained to him that he must hold still and look at Gus for the next one, but it happened again. He could only look away from his small charge for a moment without wanting to look back at him, saying "Richard, Richard," over and over to the little face.

Hawley and I had sat for nearly an hour together, talking about sports and places we came from or had been, before he brought the conversation around in the direction of the murder again. No man to be hurried was Hooker Hawley.

I had decided I liked the man, and he had apparently decided that I trusted him, which is much the same thing. I don't know if he either liked or trusted me, to be honest. He was too good a cop to let me know. But he treated me as an equal, intelligent human being, not some mere goddam civilian who had to be waded through to get his job done properly.

"What's this again about your adventure, shall we call it, in Santa Fe before you came here?"

Christ. He had been picking up bits. Now it was time to see which ones fit with which other ones.

"Who gave you Santa Fe for a piece of the puzzle?"

"Your almost landlady down in Ottery St. Mary, Mrs. Gilbert. Told me you were blown to bits by a bomb, according to her sister, who's married to a policeman, mind you, and that you're all kinds of a spy as well as an imposter who, would you believe it, never heard—"

"—of Samuel Taylor Coleridge." We finished the sentence together. "Yes, I remember Mrs. Gilbert."

"When young Howe finally told us what you had said, offhanded, he said, to be sure, about your own house back in the States being broken into, I went down there and had a word with her. Loves policemen, she does. Told me ten times how much. Can't do enough for them, she says. I thought she was going to prune me and water me and put me in a pot before she was through. Everything but useful information, that one is offering."

I gave him a synopsis of my so-called Santa Fe adventure, with as coherent an explanation as I could of how I happened to have been involved briefly with the CIA and the FBI. He raised both eyebrows at that.

"And is it a fact, then, that it was the CIA that paid your fare to fly first class over here to Raleigh?"

"It's a fact grievously subject to misinterpretation."

"Ah. Yes."

"It was a sort of apology and goodwill gesture, I think, for what they considered my help. I wish to God they had forgotten it and let me pay my own fare tourist. You're the second one to try to make something of that."

He was instantly alert in a way he had not been before. He hadn't moved a muscle, but I knew he was listening more intently then. His slow and relaxed technique had finally led me to say something he could hook onto.

"And who would the first one be?"

"You're not going to believe this one, even if you did the last."

"Try me." He picked up our two mugs. "When I get back with another drink for us." He went over to the bar and had two more drawn and paid for them. When he came back and put them down on the cloth, he went over to the fireplace and poked the fire with a tongs to liven it up before sitting back down.

"The Chinese Minister of Cultural Affairs."

"Try that one again. I thought you said the Chinese Minister of Cultural Affairs, is it?"

"Got it in one. A man named Li Chen, although when we were boys together he was called Francis Li."

"Boys together. Did he grow up in your neighborhood or you in his?"

It was a shrewd question, no conclusions leaped to.

"I grew up in China. At least from the time I was seven until I was twelve. Nineteen thirty-two to thirty-seven."

"Hmph. We're the same age. April eleventh?"

"April eighteenth."

"I'm a week older. Mind your manners."

I told him about how Gus and Francis and I had got to know each other, and how we had met again just recently.

"Amazing coincidence, when you think of it."

"Or not, if you think of it that way."

"You've got the suspicious mind of a born cop."

"But I haven't the temperament. Or guts, or whatever it is that lets you keep at it for years, never quite winning the war, always another bunch of thugs to deal with. The 'lads,' as Sergeant Pride calls them."

"I suppose it is like a war. One battle after another."

He shifted uneasily and scratched behind his ear. It was the first time I had seen him embarrassed. "I've found that whatever I say in our language to an American is going to sound pompous, the way we express things. But the simple fact is, you've got to soldier on and do the best you can, never mind the filth and the rotten swine you deal with every day. Someone's got to, anyway."

He drank a long swallow of his pint with some embarassment.

I returned to his original implied question. "I can't figure out how much of it is coincidence and how much is just one lunacy on top of another."

I took a long breath and a swallow of my own beer and tried to think of a place to start. The beginning seemed best. Beginning last week, anyway.

"I ran into Gus at the inn, and one thing led to another, and there it was, a place for me to live."

I told him about meeting Susan and Richard, and my

role in the christening. His eyes never left my face.

And I told him how I had run into Francis in the kite shop in London, and how that had led to the reunion for the three of us at the Legation Hotel. He never took a note, but I knew nothing was being forgotten, not a name or a date or a comment.

Finally, I told him of my fantastic conversation with Francis at my apartment, the whole of it, from his unexpected arrival to his frightening remark as he left.

Hooker Hawley sat back and wiped his mouth on the back of his hand. "Whew. Quite a tale."

"I'd be afraid or ashamed to tell it to most men."

"A stranger's easier, isn't it? Cops and barmen and priests behind a grill. I'll tell a strange doctor things I won't even admit to my own man about my prostate. Damned embarrassing to be asked if you still piss a good strong stream, if you have trouble turning it off, so on."

Middle-aged man's chat. More of Hooker Hawley's grounding the loose ends of the case in a handy reality. Letting the Yank professor know that after thirty years in his trade, nothing was unbelievable, nothing beyond the limits of the human nature his job had taught him.

"It's so crazy. On the one hand there is a man who I think is serious, completely sincere, who is after me about this so-called formula, and he thinks and talks of millions and hundreds of millions, of lives and money. On the other is my friend with a dead child, and two friends of his dead, too, and a broken boat I paid eight pounds forty for. And it is the dead child and the broken red boat I dream about when I can sleep."

Hawley said nothing.

16

AT MY REQUEST Hawley had taken me to Gus's house and walked me through the scene of the carnage. Gus had not returned to the site except the one time the police had asked him to reenact his finding of the victims. Sue, who was still hospitalized in grief and shock, refusing to talk to anyone, even to Gus, would probably never set foot there again.

There was a single blue and white panda car in the yard. Sergeant Pride was inside it, and he got out and greeted us in his remarkable baritone whisper when we drove up.

"Sir. Professor."

"We're just here for a look around, John."

"I'll be here, sir, if you need me."

"You on until four, then? Parsons after you?"

They talked shop for a minute about shifts and standing orders.

Hawley took me to the spot where Gus and Sue had parked after coming back from Mass. We walked through a sort of breezeway between the two long wings of the house and entered the kitchen.

The floor was still chalked, and the floor and walls and counter were still bloodstained. He showed me where Libby's body had lain, partially under the table. The chair she must have been sitting in was thrown aside and tipped over.

There was a thick trail of blood smeared across the tile floor and out the door leading back to the drive-in area. Robert had crawled, falling and sprawling and lurching in his progress, out through the door and across the yard. His bloody, blundering progress was easy to follow through the muddy turf, and in addition the police had run a double line of string marking the path.

"He must have chased the buggers along here. After the baby, I suppose, from what you all tell me. Trying to get the baby back from them."

He pointed to a marked-off spot crossing the gill and including a small part of the opposite bank. "The child's body was there. Thrown down hard, apparently, not just dropped, face down in the mud and water. And the little boat, too. Smashed down it was. Had to be to break it, a good piece of wood. Ah, but you gave that to him. You know."

"Why did they take the child?"

"We'd like the answer to that."

"If it was a kidnapping . . . But if it was, why would they change their minds—if they had any."

"If they had any is right."

"And throw him down here deliberately?"

Hawley said, "It's a funny thing, that bit of vandalism in the Brown Cottage at Mrs. Gilbert's place."

"What? Oh, that? Why? What does that have to do with this?"

"Yes, that's a question, isn't it? It was my man John Pride who mentioned it first, this. The similarity. When those fellows ripped up the cottage, they were apparently looking for something. Signs of a search, even one as clumsy as that, are pretty easy to identify. But the only thing they took was a couple of the boy's stamp-collecting books. Nothing valuable, mind, just the kind of thing kids get started doing for a lark, then quit after it gets boring."

I thought of my father's notebooks.

"Then, almost as soon as they stepped out of the door, they tossed the stamp books into the brook there. Threw them, hard. One of them was lodged in a bush across the other side."

Now I could see what Pride had seen.

"Now look at this bit of savagery here." Hawley looked back at the house. "They run out of that door there after slashing and stabbing the woman and the poor lad, and they grab up the child. We can't tell, but we think the boy might have been holding him. He had the child's blanket in his hands. The woman had just put a bottle of baby formula into the pan on the cooker to warm it. Maybe the lad was given the baby to hold, you both said he liked that. Something he could do well, I suppose.

"We think there must have been two of them. Three, possibly, one in the car who never got out. Say two. They enter the house through that door the first time. Do they expect to find anyone at home? Perhaps. A neighbor down the lane says there was a green Ford van parked down in the turnaround Sunday morning when she drove to Mass. That would get itself noticed here."

We walked slowly back toward the house, skirting the pegged-out area. Sergeant John Pride watched us, leaning on the roof of the police car.

"Let us assume that they thought the Van Durens had gone off to church, or wherever, taking the child with them. There was no other car here. It appears that Mr. Van Duren had driven the Grandisson woman and the lad over from the Exmouth train station on Saturday afternoon. Her car is in the shop up in London with dicey brakes. There was a return ticket for both of them in her purse.

"So, they are inside the house, but the two villains in the green van don't know that. So they park in the yard here, and in they go. And they run into the unexpected in the kitchen. Panic. Grab the knife . . . you know all the rest."

"But why did they go into the house in the first place?"

Hawley cocked an eyebrow as if remembering that he had asked himself that question once. "Oh, we know that, too."

He traced a path in the air with his forefinger. "The blood was tracked by one of them upstairs to the study on the first floor. They took something from there."

"My trunk." I blurted it out with a sense of anticipated horror confirmed. *My* trunk.

"It seems likely, from what you've told me. They shifted it downstairs, scoring the wallpaper as they went, and carried it right through the kitchen and out here again. The forensic laboratory lads say the van weighed some fifteen stone more driving away than coming in. It rained like bloody hell here the previous night, so there were plenty of tracks. They didn't seem to give a damn."

It was stupidly, horribly fascinating to keep staring at the paths they had walked, carrying the trunk, carrying the baby, and each time I viewed them realizing a little more that two human beings had carried all that out as part of a day's work, a job. I wanted to turn away from it and couldn't. My godson had died here, my best friend's child.

"Which . . . ?" The question choked in my throat.

"We think that they did all the killings first, and then stole the trunk. The muck on the stair treads had mud from the bank of the gill in it as well as blood."

Hawley's eyes looked at the scene for perhaps the hundredth time, still searching. They were like ice.

"The killings could have been entirely incidental. An unimportant sidelight. It was the trunk they were after; to them it was the important thing."

"If I hadn't come here, none of this might have happened."

"We don't know that, Neil, do we?"

It was the first time he had used my name.

"We'd better find out, hadn't we?"

"Perhaps it would be the next thing to talk to someone up in London, between the jigs and the reels." He seemed to say it with the greatest possible reluctance.

"My mother used to say that."

We were walking back to his car. He gave a sketchy salute to John Pride.

"My mother was from Donegal."

"Mine was from Waterford."

All the way back to Raleighston we talked about how our mothers had met our fathers and how many brothers and sisters we had.

Susan Van Duren spoke for the first time on Thursday, to Gus. She asked him to take her somewhere else. He knew what she meant, that she wanted to leave the hospital, but never return to their home in Raleigh's Gill.

136

"Edwina has offered us her house in St. Leonard's Terrace. We'll go there if that's all right with you, darling."

"Yes. There. Soon, please." For the first time, too, she wept, tears starting to well up and then pouring from her eyes. She lifted her arms to him and he held her, half sitting on the bed.

"Don't be gentle, Gus, hug me hard, please," she groaned to him, sobbing and rocking him. Each was in the other's arms, each was the comforter. She would be well now, Gus knew, and he was fiercely glad. He had thought he'd never feel gladness again.

I was called by the hospital on Friday morning and told that I could visit with them in Sue's room, but that I should come in through the Emergency entrance and ask for Sister More.

She was a tall, thin, no-nonsense nurse. She told me, as we zigzagged our way back through the hospital corridors to the opposite wing, that her brother, Bobby More, was the Detective Chief Inspector in charge of the region. That meant he was Hooker Hawley's boss. I had seen his name in the papers, saying that the crime would not be solved overnight. Someone must issue those meaningless press releases, I suppose, and I know that Hooker was glad it wasn't him. Maybe that was why he was still only a detective inspector at his age and experience.

Gus shook my hand with his two and Sue sat up to give me a hug. She was still chalky white, and her eyes were sunken into blue rings of exhaustion, but her hair was freshly combed, and she was disconnected from the hospital apparatus they had been using to feed her.

We talked about Edwina's house, which was, from their embarrassed description, a great, sprawling, six-bedroom townhouse overlooking Burton Court, with a separate garden flat for the help and enough clocks to fill a museum wing.

"It's terribly *Town and Country*, but we shall only stay there until we can get a new place of our own," Gus said mournfully.

"It's exactly what we left London to get away from," Sue

said. "Really, it's shaming, too grandly sterile to be believed. And Edwina's clocks give it the air of a stately home, open on Thursdays for thirty p."

"Sue drew the line at keeping the cook and man Edwina offered us."

They didn't have to explain that they wanted only each other for a while, or why.

Gus asked me to go with him up to London to make funeral arrangements. Although Sue became a shade paler, we talked about that. They had obviously agreed that they had to get on with living, as decently and as intelligently as they could, and they exchanged one glance and Gus held her hand while we talked it through.

Richard had died of suffocation in the mud of the stream bank, Gus told me.

We did not discuss the crimes, only about the fact of the three deaths and what must be done next.

"Neil," Sue said, stretching out her hand to touch mine, "you musn't think me cruel to say this, but Gus told me about your Pril and how she died. We think that, better than anyone else, you understand how we feel now."

I squeezed her hand. "Yes. In part, at least. Thank you." For the first time I felt my own tears coming. We got back to making plans for their move to London.

17

THE DAYS AND the hours in them became a weary blur. I walked the cliff path to Exmouth in one direction, six miles of red mud and stiles to clamber over and heart-stopping views down from the cliffs to the sea. Then, foot-sore and aching, with mud caked on my sneakers and splattered on my suntans, I sat in a pub for two hours and drank three Jameson's and watched the customers play the complicated slot machine that paid off a grand prize of £2 for two pence. The bus took me back to Raleighston, but not to rest. The next morning, having slept parts of each hour for five, I put on fresh wool socks and crammed my still wet sneakers back on and walked in the other direction even farther to Sidmouth and repeated the day.

There was no rain, and the wind was constant from the sea, southerly. Each morning the sun would rise through soft, screening fog and then burn brightly for an hour, and then be seen only fitfully through a layer of low cloud. Often it would break suddenly through a rift and pour down like a benediction on a single wide spot over the water.

My book was a lost cause. My notes seemed stale and stupid, and if I sat at my typewriter the blank paper mocked my sense of my own dullness. My mind ached for the lost ease of thought and phrase. I was like a runner in slow quicksand, not moving, only straining and sinking.

Donne had written once, "The world is all in pieces, all coherence gone." It was true.

When the feeling was growing in me increasingly that I could do nothing in the wake of this immense pain to my friends, I called Oldhampton again because it seemed to be doing something, and talked with Chief Scalli.

He, naturally, knew nothing of the current situation in

Raleighston, and so I limited my questions to his investigation of my house burglary back home.

"Any more news about what, for Chrissakes, Professor?"

"The theft of my trunk and the slugging of my house-sitter."

"News he calls it. I told you we found the trunk and all that. Down Dombrowski's onion farm?"

"Yes, you told me that before."

"Yeah, well, last—what, Tuesday, Wednesday, wait a minute, I'll check the book—Wednesday it was, Curran over in Northampton picked up an abandoned van matching the description your boy Bradley gave us of the one the two comedians were using. Could be the same one. Reason I think so, there was a model ship, exactly like the other ones in that trunk we brought in, in the back. All smashed to hell, but you know, same kind of material and all that."

Coincidence was one thing, but that was too strange to have any real connection.

"We figure the guys drove the van someplace empty, like Dombrowski's over there behind the big storage sheds, and went through the trunk to see if it had whatever it was they were after. No dice, so into the ditch it goes. But either this toy ship doesn't get put back in or one of them just took it out and then left it in the truck. We got one funny ID from a lady in Northampton."

"What's funny about it?"

"They left the van over behind the Peter Pan bus station there. I figure they must've climbed on a bus to Boston or New York. We asked everyone we could locate who took a bus there that night, anytime between eight and the last bus, eleven thirty, did they see these two guys, one big, one little. Driver says he can't remember all the clowns get on there. Ticket guy says same thing. But they both say this little old German lady gets on the late bus three times a week, to Springfield. So we track her down. Mrs. Grundfel or something like that, I got it here in the book. One of these nosy old bitches makes a good witness because she's watching everybody else all the time. She identifies everybody on the bus for us. Including two guys she calls no-goods, never on that bus before. And before I can even ask her anything about them, this will kill you, she starts to hold her nose. Then she starts pointing in her mouth and says, 'roast' and 'fry' over and over. I figure, Jesus, one of these guys must look like Colonel Sanders, you know, the fried-chicken guy. So I'm yelling for Moran to get his ass out of the car and get over there, because he had two years of German in high school, and the old broad's yelling 'roast, fry' with her finger in her mouth and it's like a fucking Chinese fire drill until Moran tells me it's the German for stainless steel. One of these bozos has got a stainless steel tooth, for Chrissakes. That and B.O., I guess."

"Is that all?"

"Listen, that's a lot. Moran even showed her his spoon from his lunchbag to be sure. He won't eat his yogurt with a plastic spoon, a gourmet. She says, 'Ya, ya, like dat,' pointing to the stainless steel spoon. We finally tape-recorded her statement and got Rosenberg, the German teacher up the high school, to translate it. That's what she said. Scared the shit out of her, I guess, because she kept saying, 'Roosian, Roosian have dat.' I guess she's more afraid of the Roosians than of anything else, so she remembered this guy pretty good."

Everything Francis had said to me flooded back. But at transatlantic prices I knew that I didn't need to think of it now. Scalli was perfectly willing to talk forever; he wasn't paying for the call.

"I thought you promised me you wouldn't fool around with those spies anymore, Professor. What's this, you got some stainless-steel Russian trying to steal your poetry books now?"

I hung up on him while he was still enjoying his own humor.

Hooker Hawley would be interested in that.

The man with the steel tooth was no Russian. Hooker knew that immediately.

141

"Good Christ," he snorted when I started to tell him about Scalli's German woman. "Good Almighty Christ in heaven. They sent a couple of locals."

I asked him what he meant.

"If there's a Russian answering that description I imagine it's no great coincidence, statistically. But it makes more sense to me to think that the two dickies who did your house in Massachusetts were London lads. Murph and Davey Bishop. Murph has a tin tooth and a pong like rotten fish. Davey likes to cut people."

We were in Hawley's car, on our way to London to meet some new players in the game.

I still don't know which British police service was represented by the three men we met with in the office on St. James Place in London—Special Branch or SAS or MI5 or Slithy Toves, Inc. And no one offered to fill me in.

Hooker Hawley and I had entered the building, a modernized Regency gem with a carpeted lobby and an elevator with a directory on the wall next to it. Hawley had found the address only after consulting another doorway himself, so I knew that he wasn't exactly on familiar ground.

"Mr. Marbury, if you please," he said genially to the elevator man, who appeared to my eye to be no old pensioner working at a cushy job. More like a retired cop or marine, still fit, jacket buttoned down nicely over a meaty frame. And perhaps a gun that he was perfectly prepared to use.

He took us without speaking to the top floor and opened the door for us. We stepped out into a foyer at right angles to a waist-high counter stretching across wall to wall. Behind it stood another large, imposing character in buttoned jacket and navy tie. The elevator man stayed in the open door beside us. I think it is called an enfilade. Those doing the shooting are in no danger of hitting each other.

The wide one behind the counter grinned with great brown teeth. "Hayer, Hooker? They told me you'd be popping in. Got them, William," he said to his twin in the elevator, who only then closed his door and left.

142

Hawley reached over the counter. "Bernard. How's it? Long time."

"Eight years, Hook. The Casey mob in Birmingham."

"This is Neil Kelly; Bernard King. Old chum of mine from a century back. Pal from America, Bernard."

I was offered a hand the size of a ham to shake.

I accepted the implied compliment of being introduced by name without title. I was sure Bernard understood the shorthand, too. He relaxed just enough for it to be noticeable and nearly destroyed my hand shaking it.

"We're here to see your Mr. Marbury."

"So it says in my book. You're four minutes early. He wouldn't see God four minutes early. He's got a dolly of a secretary, though. Would you rather look at her or talk with me?"

"Look at her, of course, but what the hell. How's Helen and the girls? I lived in Bernard's house once for a year," he said in an aside to me.

"Helen's fine. Bit of the arthritis now in her hands. She takes these herbs are supposed to relieve it. I don't know if they do or not. Jen's got three kids now, Claire's two are out of school already, the pair of them. They think they're Teds or something."

"Jen's got three of her own? Christ, I still think of her this high, always taking care of Claire's."

"Yes, well, she married a nice lad from Reading, works for the British Rail. Talks a lot about going on strike, does Charles, but he's a good worker, takes good care of Jen."

A door opened behind Bernard and a young woman with large glasses looked out and said, "Room Three, Bernard, darling."

He tilted his head toward her as she shut the door. "That's her. Dolly Varden. I'm her secret fancy man. Room Three's that side. I'll ring and you can lift the flap there and go on in."

"Watchit, Bernard." Hawley shot him with a finger.

"Watchit, Hooker."

We edged through the flap in the counter and went into Room Three.

I thought that maybe I'd already heard about Bernard without his name coming into it.

On the ride up from Devon Hawley had told me a lot more about his career and added a few footnotes about his nickname. Five years as a vice cop in London before he transferred out to the provinces at his own request.

"Are you a big-city man, back in the States, Neil?"

"Uh uh. I've lived in small towns, academic towns most of my life. The only time I lived in the city was when I was a graduate student."

"It would be hard for a man to credit if he hadn't actually lived there. I grew sick of it. Not just tired of it, the noise, the pollution, that lark, you know. I began getting sick from the people we had to deal with. Scum scraped off your shoe. People who had turned themselves to shit and wanted to turn everyone else the same thing." He drove in silence for a full mile.

"Decided to kill myself then. Maybe I'd've done it, too, but a friend of mine prevented me. I was going off to drown myself, how do you like that for drama? Drove myself down to the coast just above Lyme Regis. Sat on the damned beach all night crying like a baby. Too scared to walk in and too scared to go back. My friend and I used to go fishing down there, kept a little hacker of a boat on the beach. I turned it over and lay down in it—it was named the *Belle*, that was his choice, we flipped a tanner to see who'd name it—and I slept in it until he leaned his big mug in there and pulled me out the next morning. Worried about me, he said. Thought maybe I'd decided to go fishing alone.

"We took the boat out, the two of us omadhans, and rowed our guts out down the coast and back, halfway to Cornwall.

" 'This bit of coast wouldn't be a bad place to be a cop, Hooker,' he says. It was the first time I got it through my thick head I could be a cop and not be a city cop, a vice cop especially, anymore.

144

"Been out here away from the smoke since about then. Smartest dumb thing I ever did."

"Did you catch any fish?"

"Not a one. Some hooker you are, my mate says."

He drove without speaking then for more than one mile.

"It was the girls, mostly, I minded. You had girls, right? The young ones, hookers, of course, and I got plenty of guff about that in my time. Twelve, thirteen, fourteen years old, hard as nails. Their mothers hookers, tarts, toms, whatever you call them. Whores. Little girls in pink wrappers in their prams and then a few years later on the street. Half them their dads done when they were still under ten. Their dads or their brothers or their Mum's boyfriend. And the drugs. And the beatings. And all of it. I can still feel it in my gut if I want to think about it. The hopelessness of them."

"My mother used to say 'omadhan,' too. To me, as a matter of fact," I said.

He laughed. "Did you ever ask her what it meant, exactly?"

"Of course."

"And what did she say?"

"She said an omadhan is the first cousin to an oonshook."

He pounded the steering wheel with his hand and roared. "I knew it. So did mine, so did mine. The first cousin to an oonshook."

Room Three in St. James Place was simply an office. It might have been any bank meeting room, the kind where my partner and I, Hawley and Kelly, Inc., might be interviewed for a bank loan against our inventory of vacuum cleaners and toasters.

The three men seated around the rectangular table facing us were not bankers. Even British bankers could not have looked that pessimistic about the prospects of our loan.

Marbury spoke first and greeted us by name.

"Detective Inspector Hawley, I believe, and this must be Mr. Kelly from Washington."

145

Hawley did our talking. I didn't know whether to phone or get out of the booth.

"Mr. Marbury. You understand, Mr. Kelly is here with me at the request of the Foreign Office, liaising with Washington."

Marbury nodded mutely. If he didn't know it, you can bet he wasn't going to admit it to Hawley. The man on his left took a note. Kelly was on another list of American spies, I suppose.

"The gentleman on my left is Geoffrey Haddon. My exec, so to speak, Mr. Kelly," a millisecond of smile, "and on my right, Anthony Kelland. How can we assist you?"

We seated ourselves without invitation in the only two chairs available. Hooker took his time before beginning.

"You have my brief concerning Li Chen, the Chinese national."

Three economical nods.

"Mr. Kelly knows Li Chen personally. Knew him as a child, when his name was Francis Li. He will tell you a rather complicated story concerning Francis Li or Li Chen, and then we shall have a request to make."

The three musketeers managed not to leap from their seats with whoops of joy when they heard that Professor Kelly was going to conduct a seminar for them. So did Professor Kelly. I looked witheringly at my companion, who ignored me with the ease of a man who has been withered by experts.

It really wasn't all that different from a hundred presentations I had made in the past thirty years to faculty committees or trustee committees or grant committees of foundations. Three men were seated in front of me who didn't particularly want to hear whatever I had to impart. They had something that we wanted, although Hooker had not told me what it was. My job was simply to convince them that they had been overlooking one of life's golden opportunities in not having given it to us long before this.

Marbury fancied himself suave. He liked to finger his guardsman's moustache while he was listening, which enabled him to droop the corners of his mouth sarcastically without actually appearing to hold you in contempt. Just the suspicion of contempt.

Haddon was his personal sycophant. He was as tuned to his mentor's wavelength as the finest education in discipleship could have made him. He let a fractional smile play about his lips at the amusing prospect of hearing an actual American speak.

Kelland looked like an eager young graduate student waiting for the question on his orals. Whatever it was he was going to pounce on it and tear it to pieces. He might even get it right. But he would not reflect on it, he would attack it. He had been winning prizes and scholarships all his life with that technique, and now his teeth were practically bared in readiness.

I felt strangely at home. As plainly as I could, with a minimum of howdy do's and you betcha's, I told them the story of Sir Edmund Backhouse, of Our Gang, and of my father's notebooks.

Haddon took enough notes to constitute a memoir. When I had finished, some twenty minutes later, Marbury lifted his gaze from the table, fixed it on me and spoke.

"Interesting. One might almost say fascinating. Sir Edmund Backhouse, of course, we know. A remarkable historical figure." Figgah. "Li Chen we know only as an apparently minor figure"—figgah—"in the Embassy of the Chinese People's Republic."

A tacit rebuke to my sloppy nomenclature. Shucks, now I wished I had said "Red China."

"The F.O. confirm his prior activities and record of political favor and disfavor inside the People's Republic. What would you have us do?"

Back to square one. All trustees dealing with mere faculty know the gambit. As soon as the poor fish makes his ablest presentation, let him think that he still hasn't said anything.

Hooker spoke up. "We have hard evidence that Li Chen, this inferior minister of the People's Republic of China, might be connected with a triple murder which took place down in Devon this past weekend."

Marbury murmured a sympathetic something, the burden of which was that he knew my godchild had been one of the victims and he was indeed sorry. He had been well briefed, probably by Haddon, who looked like the dog whose master had just won best in show.

"From this point forward," Hooker went on, "we should like to liaise with you every step of the way."

"They love to liaise," he had said to me in the car. "Bloody buggers would rather liaise than anything else going."

Marbury let a smile rich in cholesterol spread itself across his pink features. "We thought you might. That. Is. Why. Anthony Kelland. Is. Here."

We all swiveled to look at our degree candidate, who bared his teeth in delight and to show readiness.

"Mr. Kelland speaks Chinese." Marbury couldn't have been prouder of his little coup than if he had produced the goose that laid the golden eggs.

I wanted Hooker to be proud of me, otherwise I'd never have asked Kelland, in Chinese, which dialects he spoke.

He paled slightly, but answered in reasonably good graduate-school Cantonese that he had learned Chinese in Hong Kong, and that Cantonese was about as far as his knowledge went.

"No north coastal dialects?" I asked him, in Cantonese, apparently askance.

None.

"And no Mandarin?" We were dealing, I reminded him in the wonderful scolding tones of the Chinese schoolmaster I had heard so often myself, with a man of the capital, of Peking.

He confessed a total inability to manage the northern dialects.

I didn't want to destroy him, but I thought it might be a useful lesson for him to hear just a bit more.

"You don't by any chance have any of the Sinkiang dialects, do you, or Manchurian?"

No, sir, he didn't. Well, neither do I, except for some restaurant Manchurian, have any of them except Cantonese

148

about as good as Anthony Kelland's, some Fukien, fluent Mandarin, and bits and pieces of some coastal patois, but there was no one in that room who was going to find that out.

"Perhaps you'd like to explain to Mr. Marbury, Mr. Kelland, what we were just discussing."

He looked stricken. Marbury, for his part, was as plumped up as a mother at a piano recital of her champion offspring. His moustache drooped dramatically when he saw that all was not going well with his protégé's Chinese performance.

Kelland explained with impressive dignity that he had just failed his oral exam. That, indeed, the American gentleman was fluent in forms of Chinese approximately one light-year beyond him.

I was as nice as my nasty streak — which tends to come out in the presence of arrogant and pompous fools — permitted me to be.

"Perhaps you were unaware, Mr. Marbury, that I grew up *in China*. It was there that Francis Li and I were boys together, not in America or Hong Kong."

"I see. Remarkable. Naturally, I assumed."

Hooker, to whose wavelength I was increasingly becoming attuned, was in heaven. I didn't dare look at him.

He knew it was exactly his moment to take the ball. When he finished explaining what he wanted to do now, the musketeers left the room briefly to confer. When they returned, they were two plus one. Kelland had been benched. They brought in a satiric-looking Welshman named Jones. He, it seemed, would be liaising with us, not the polyglot Kelland. He looked like a good tough man.

Now Hooker had all his bases covered and he couldn't have been sunnier. Back in the car he hummed under his breath — "Limehouse Blues," I think, although I couldn't swear it, he was so tone deaf — and told me we were ready now to move. Will Storey, his old partner from the C.I.D., would be our point man on one side, liaising, as he said deliciously, with the Yard, and Jones on the other. Hooker

149

in the center would run the show, although each of the others would probably believe he was running it.

"You're full of guile, Hooker."

"Me? I'm a schoolboy compared with you, you villain. Tell me again what you said to that pasty-faced little runt in Chinese, you Yank superstar you."

18

"HE'S A BLUE-EYED smiler, our Bobby More."

Hooker was preparing me for meeting his boss, the Regional Commander *pro tem*, the man eventually responsible to the Chief Constable for the management of the murder investigation.

"The Regional Commander, who should be here, will probably be forced to retire now; back gives him hell. Poor bugger was in traction the last time I saw him, hanging up like a piece of meat. One of those things they must fuse the spine for eventually." He grunted.

"I get the impression you and Sergeant Pride prefer the other man."

"Do you. Yes, you might if I wasn't careful. Bobby should have been an M.P. Minister of Artifice."

He braked sharply and shot the car into a slot marked Reserved, with a grunt of satisfaction.

He was, as advertised, a full-fledged, glad-handing blue-eyed smiler, a politician in double-vented navy pinstripe and plump tapestry tie. He shook my hand warmly and fatly. I tried not to wince when Hooker distinctly pronounced the words "representing the White House in this" to him. The warmth, and perhaps even a little of the fatness increased.

"Oh, I see. Welcome to England, Mr. Kelly."

"Thanks." I thought perhaps a laconic style might best hide my ignorance of what was going on.

"Marbury's mob have approved this at the top level," Hooker added shamelessly, tipping his head toward the Yank.

"Of course, of course." It was obvious that he was relieved to accept me as someone else's responsibility.

Hooker spent the next twenty minutes telling Bobby More what to tell him to do, and More did it with all the ignorant and pompous sincerity of the practiced self-deluder.

More was certainly going to let Hawley do it whichever way he wanted. He was one of those superior officers just smart enough to know that one of his subordinates was a lot better at the job than he was, and just ambitious and shameless enough to let him do it. The secret is to be there when they are assigning the credit and the promotions, and Bobby More was clearly very skilled in that department.

"I only want one of Marbury's mob trailing along," Hooker told him. "And tell your friend in the Yard that it would be a very intelligent idea to assign Will Storey to this one. Tell him Will is just the man to keep this idiot Hawley from ruining the whole show, but what are you to do, he's the only Detective Inspector you've got to spare and all that bumf."

More wrote it all down, although I doubt if he got it verbatim. If I knew my bureaucrats the whole world over, he was papering his file in case the whole operation went down the tube. The memorandum would show that Hawley was responsible for all the errors of judgment, More for the prudent provisions.

We left there with a brief to carry on exactly as Hooker wanted. Bobby More pounced from his swivel chair to press his fat hand to mine once more. Hooker was conveniently busy with his coat.

"Well," Bobby beamed, " 'England expects,' eh? Nelson, Mr. Kelly, Lord Nelson. 'England expects every man to do his duty.' Something I always like to quote when we have an operation starting. Doesn't mean anything, really, a sort of good-luck saying, includes even the Americans, I suppose, eh?"

"We quote it often, Chief Inspector," I told him, looking him right in the eye. "The whole thing."

"The whole thing? How's that, then?"

" 'England expects—I forbear to proceed. 'Tis a maxim tremendous but trite. But you'd best be preparing the things you will need to fit yourselves out for the fight.' "

"I say. Here's a Yank telling us our British history, eh, Hawley? Marvelous. Never heard that, the whole quotation, I mean."

He saw us out thoughtful and beamish.

Back in the car Hooker slammed his hand down on my knee. "Lovely. The Hunting of the bloody Snark. Lovely, just beautiful. You and I should have met years ago."

"How could we," the cowboy asked out of the side of his mouth, "if the White House didn't send me over until now?"

"Now for the snark. Or the boojum or whatever it turns out to be."

"Who's Will Storey?" I was losing track of the cast members.

"Will Storey and I worked together for a few years, too, way back. What I remember best about him is that he could stay awake for twenty-four hours at a stretch and not even blink. Then he'd take a four-hour kip and be back at it. Marvelous metabolism. Keeps his mouth shut, too. That helps in a pinch."

A pun? I was too afraid that Hooker would notice that I was still trailing his footsteps to ask. He let me know he hadn't forgotten.

"You're here because you want to be, got it? My royal red British ass will be in a sling ten feet off the ground if anything happens to you, or if the Chief Constable ever even finds out. But he was your godson, wasn't he, eh? So you're not here, but you're here if you want it."

I wanted it. I was there.

"Murph is an old lag we've all brushed up against off and on for thirty years. Thief, for the most part."

We were driving across London along the edge of Hyde Park bordered by Bayswater Road. Storey's car, a C.I.D. blue Mini, was in front of us, and somewhere behind us was the man from Marbury's company, the saturnine black-eyed Welshman named Jones.

We had rendezvoused at Paddington Station and Hooker had set out the order of battle. He had introduced me to Storey simply as Neil Kelly, representing the Yanks here, and the Yard man hadn't batted an eye. I could only guess what variety of secret services he and Jones assigned me to in their heads. Hooker was a fearless liar.

Storey was to come up and hold the fort outside Murphy's room while Hooker and Kelly went in. Jones was the street man. Assuming that our quarry was tucked in bed where he belonged at three in the morning, it would be what my students would call "a piece of cake."

"What do you think, Neil? Are we going to nail him or is this whole thing going to come apart at the seams and leave us looking like damn fools?"

"A piece of cake, Hooker."

He laughed immoderately. "Jesus. You American cops sure talk tough."

"Why the steel tooth? I'm like Scalli, I thought only the Russians had steel teeth."

"You'll not see many this side, that's sure. A mob of tearaways back in the sixties made it their trademark. True. They all had one steel tooth put in. They got the idea from some James Bond film or some such nonsense. It didn't last long. There were about nine or ten of them. Murph was one of the middle-level lads. Three of them got themselves killed trying to run away from a bank job in Hampstead ten years back. Probably five of them are inside at the moment, so Will tells me, and he should know. Murph and his mate Davey Bishop are the last of them, so it was an easy guess and then just a matter of asking the right people the right questions."

We were suddenly where Hooker wanted to be, on a half-lit street in Soho. Jones must have passed us at some point, because he was parked in front of a restaurant with his hand out the window, thumb up. That meant he was in front of the building we'd enter.

Hooker found a place to park fifty yards along. I had a sudden dramatic increase of pulse and a dry mouth. I got out of my side anyway, against all my civilian instincts, and swallowed as hard as I could, knowing that if I had to speak, I'd squeak.

No one asked me to. Hooked walked back to Jones's Mini, where Will Storey was already standing waiting.

The three of us went to the doorway next to the restaurant and Storey had it open about as quickly as I can unlock my own front door. He flashed a pocket flashlight up the dirty, steep stairs and took them two at a time, catlike. Hooker went next, one step at a time, just as quietly, and I brought up the rear, feeling as though I were wearing snowshoes and making enough racket in my own ears to feel like a damned fool. I might as well have worn boots and spurs; they were probably thinking Christ, here comes the Seventh Cavalry. No wonder Custer got massacred.

"He'll talk. He'll fucking sing, you watch," Hooker had said. "Murph is a thief, not a frightener or a hard man with a gun. He thinks he's some kind of poor-man's cat burglar, and he has a bad flaw. Two of them, actually, and I'm going to use one to get at the other. I'm going to lean on him so hard he will want to tell me the dirtiest secrets he has. Talk your damned ear off, will friend Murph if you get him started. Fear starts him, fear and pain. He actually likes it. One of those dickies gets himself flogged by a tart when he has enough to afford it. He's going to love me when I'm through with him. He'll fucking well adore me."

I had to shudder. Hooker Hawley was taking himself right back down into the dark place which he had finally almost escaped from in suicide. Down into the region of the human soul where there was no longer any contest between good and evil, only the rot of evil in possession.

"Have you ever seen an exorcism, Neil?"

"Only in the movies."

"Believe in it?"

"Oh, yes. I've no doubt some get possessed by evil."

"I've seen some. They come out with a terrible stink, actually. Mephitic. Evil really does stink."

He shook his head as if to clear it from a remembered vision.

"Murph stinks. All the time. Pong you could slice with a knife. The German woman noticed it, didn't she? When your man Scalli said she described the man on the bus as stinking filthy and flashing a steel tooth, I didn't have much doubt who it might be. And he admires cruelty.

"Has a mate, Murph has. Davey Bishop. The Bishop, they call him. Mean little weasel. A hurter. Likes to hurt. Animals and so on. Not very brave. Murph lets him put cigarettes on him, that sort of thing, real chums."

I was miles outside my native boundaries, and I was becoming more aware of it every second.

Blundering up those stairs and standing in the reeking hallway at the top, listening without breathing while Hooker tapped on the door with the tips of his fingers and whispering, "Murph, Murph, Arthur sent me. It's important," I could hear my own heart hammering against my ribs.

The door opened a crack and that was all Hooker and Storey needed. Murph, who had been standing half-awake in his underwear with his eye to the door, caught the full force of it in his face when the two of them smashed it back into him. He was half spun around and hurled across the bed he had just left, blood pouring down his face.

Hooker put on the light and Will Storey shut the door and put his back against it long enough to see that everything was under control, then he went out quietly. Kelly, representing the Seventh Cavalry, stood like an omadhan against the wall and watched. Murph, at least, seemed impressed. His eyes kept darting from Hooker to me and back. Finally he bawled, through the snot and blood he was mopping from himself with the bedclothes, "Hey, Hooker, hey. Who's he, Hooker? Whaddya want, Hooker? I didn't do nothing, you know, Hooker. Who's he? What's he here for? You don't need him, Hooker."

He was unshaven for at least three days and he and the room stank of everything. There was food on the bed and on the floor, stale crusts, empty cans, and beer bottles everywhere. It had been a filthy, dull little room to begin with, and he had been hiding in it long enough to turn it into a sewer.

"He's the godfather of the baby you murdered, you piece of shit, and I've told him that after I'm through with you he can do anything he wants to you."

"Aw, no, Hooker. Don't do that. What, Hooker, I never did no baby. What are you talking about, man?"

"I'll make one bargain with you, Murph, you ugly pile of dogshit with your tin tooth. If you answer my questions right, I'll take you in and you'll get whatever the judge gives you. Wrong and you'll never leave this toilet. Because you'll die right here."

"I gotta piss, Hooker. Let me piss first."

"Piss in your pants if you want to, Murph, but don't move one fucking inch. You and your mate did that baby, didn't you? And the woman. And the boy."

It was a challenge, not a question. The man crouched on the bed, pawing at his nose with the sodden bedclothes, risked a glance at me, and then cringed back when Hooker snarled at him.

"No, no. You got it all wrong. I'm a thief, Hooker, you know that. I never done nobody in my life."

"We've got you dead to your fucking British rights, Murph. For the American job and for the job at Ottery."

"Aw, Hooker. What American job? That was a lark, like. That wasn't no job." He had stopped the blood from flowing and was pushing himself against the back of the bed, taking some kind of a stand. It was like watching an animal at bay back toward the wall.

"Who was the bright boy with you? Was it our old chum Davey?"

"Aw, no, not Davey, Hooker. That was someone else."

Hooker had let him get just confident enough, just settled enough into his favorite kind of cat-and-mouse, question-and-answer game. He walked over to him and cold-bloodedly hit him across the nose with the edge of his hand. This time it broke, and the blood and mucus ran down in a new torrent over the man's chest and he screamed like an animal.

"I was there, Hooker, but I never lifted a finger. I never.

Jesus, you're killing me. Freddy done it. Aw, Jesus, Hooker, you've got to get him and put him someplace, he's as crazy as a fucking army of nuts. Aw, Jesus, I'm bleeding to death." He blew his broken nose horribly into the sheet and cried and hugged himself at the pain.

"Tell me about it." Hooker was not moved by a show he had probably seen a hundred times. Directed a hundred times.

"It was Freddy what sodding done it all, not me."

"Sure it was, Murph. You weren't even there."

"Come on, Hooker. I was there, I admitted that. I told you that, didn't I?"

"You've told me sod all, Murph. Sweet F.A. is what you've told me, and as far as I'm concerned, you and Freddy are the same thing. Identical."

"Aw, come on now, Hooker."

"Detective Inspector Hawley to you, you little pisspot tuppenny turd."

"Aw. All right, then, Inspector—"

"Detective Inspector Hawley. Try it. Don't speak to me unless you say it. And put a 'sir' on it, you goddammed nothing." Hooker's ice-cold brutality even frightened me.

"Aw. I thought we went back a long way, Detective Inspector, you and me. Sir, I mean."

"We started today, you and me, Murph. I don't want even to be in the same room with you, let alone have you claiming me for your mate, so shut your hole."

"Aw—"

"Shut it, I said." The eyes kept watching him, but Murph closed his mouth and chewed away at his cheek.

"Now, then. When did you and Freddy team up?"

"I dunno. Month ago, six weeks. Down in Sidmouth it was. I dunno exactly."

"Why did you? Lose Davey Bishop, did you?"

"Davey got the cancer. Fair eaten alive with it, he was. Took him off to Richmond Hill. Davey was ex-service, y'know. Army man."

"Yes, he was. Until they threw him out for abusing a

158

minor his first leave. He cut her nipples off with scissors, didn't he?"

"Aw. There was no harm in poor Davey, Hoo—"

"Shut."

"Sir."

"Where did Freddy come in?"

He shrugged. "Dunno if I remember. I can't remember everything, y'know. We struck up talking down by the shore there, behind the hotel where he was working as a caretaker, like. You know, taking a smoke, one thing and another, the way y'do."

"I can guess. You were scrounging in the dustbins for something you could eat or flog for booze and Freddy was emptying bins for the hotel, that it?"

"Yeah, well. You really know old Murph, Detective Inspector, sir, and I won't deny it."

"When did the two of you get the bright idea to team up and do a job together?"

"I swear to God, never. Never, I swear it."

"But you did."

"It was a complete surprise to me, sir, I swear to God. Out of the blue, like."

"Tell me about it."

"Well, like I said, it came out of the blue, like. I might have been a bit down on my luck, as you say, just at that particular time, but I had a very nice run, thank you, just after the first of the year. Very nice. I had over three hundred quid at one time there. Bit of luck." He grinned horribly through the mess.

"Tell me now or stand charges for it later, Murph. What did you steal that got you that kind of roll?"

"Aw. You can ask Danny Price, what took it off me. A nice piece of Georgian silver. Found it. I swear to God I found it in a bin in Kensington. Tearing the place down, they were. Must've got thrown out in the rubbish."

"We'll talk to Danny Price about it later. When it turns up stolen, Murph, that goes on the charge sheet too, you fucking liar."

"You'll see. Ask Danny. Clear title—"

"Shut it."

"Sir. But I had the lolly. I bought myself a bag of those great velvet apricots they sell. Never had none of them before. Lovely treat they are."

"So you had spent your three hundred on apricots, you lying pint of piss, and you were flat again, down in Sidmouth looking for some easy tourist to do."

"No, no, no. *I* was a tourist, don't you see? I even stayed in one of those hotels for a night. Very nice. I'd give it about two and a half stars if I was the RAC."

"They're probably still washing the linen. Name?"

"Of the hotel? The Rose, it was. Lovely place, lovely name. I plan to go back there someday."

"Forget it. When was this?"

"I won't forget that, will I? My birthday. How d'you like that? No one else was going to give old Murph a present for his fiftieth, so I says to myself, do it. Life begins at fifty, they say, y'know."

"When? A date, you moron."

"April the twenty-fifth. Nineteen-thirty-one I was born. That's why I couldn't do my service in the war, isn't it, too young. Just a baby I was."

"Just a baby. You ugly twit, if you tell me one more thing I didn't ask you, I'll stuff my boot up your ass."

"You ast me the date didn't you?" He snuffled rottenly.

"So on April the tenth you were passing yourself off as a tourist down in Sidmouth, looking about for the odd chance to make off with the lockbox and out the back and you ran into friend Freddy."

"I should have known the little bastard was queer. He was pissing in the cans of milk out by the loading door. Isn't that the most disgusting thing you ever heard? Pissing and humming away, he was. 'Hey, mate,' he says, 'wanna put yours in with mine?' "

"Turn it off, will you Murph. I don't want the Royal Shakespeare Theatre here."

"Well, it's the way he was, and I should have seen there'd

160

be worse coming. He puts his pecker away as nice as you please and offers me a smoke, and we just fall to talking about this and that, the weather, y'know, and like that."

"And Ottery St. Mary, Murph?"

He looked surprised. "Aw, that never came into it. The first thing came up was going over to the States."

"Who called you?"

"Call came down from London, see. My baby brother, Arthur. There's a coming lad, Hooker. Detective Inspector, I mean. Pride of the family is Arthur. Called me on the telephone that morning."

"Bullshit, Murph."

"Why is it?"

"Arthur wouldn't even know if you were in or out, let alone staying at The Rose down in Sidmouth. So stuff it."

"Well, I kind of called him first, see. You know young Arthur, always an eye for the next chance. When I told him—I came around his club downstairs here, he manages for Jimmy Dzu, to let him see my new suit, bit of flash so he'd know the big brother wasn't on his uppers, y'know—so I dropped a hint I might be passing through Sidmouth for a holiday. And he tells me to keep an eye out for what's going on there, any chances for young Arthur, y'see."

"All right, Murph. So you phoned Arthur to tell him you thought you saw a way of lifting the till or whatever at The Rose or maybe the place next door, and then what?"

"I swear to God, sir, you've got it all wrong. My mother's grave, nothing like that in the least."

Hooker lifted his hand again and the creature on the bed cringed and whined and covered his face with his filthy arm.

"Shut your gob."

"Sorry. This is thirsty work, Detective Inspector Hawley, sir. Any chance we might skip over there to Chinny's and have a cuppa while we talk, all nice and friendly? I'm helping you out, amn't I? Just a cuppa."

"Not a chance."

"Fag? Any brand will do."

"That's broad-minded of you, Murph. No fags, no tea, nothing but the work end of my boot up your nose if you move a goddam muscle."

"You're hard, man. Fair, but hard. I always said it."

"The States."

"Aw, did I mention that? Sure I did. So young Arthur says to me, forget all about Sidmouth, Gordy—that's what they call me in the family, y'know, Gordy, short for Gordon. Forget all about Sidmouth, Gordy, says young Arthur, and get back up here quick like. I think I've got a lovely trip laid on for you. You and Davey, he says." Hooker had been right. Murph was actually enjoying this.

"You told me Davey was in hospital with cancer."

"Of course I did. He was, wasn't he? And didn't I tell young Arthur the same? But I've got a new mate, Arthur, I said. Chap named Freddy. Seems very intelligent, very quick. Fearless bastard, I told him, not knowing how fearless old Freddy really was. How could I?"

"So Freddy had one more go at poisoning the milk with his cigarette end and the two of you went off, eh?"

"That's just what he did, too. Popped it right in on top of his piddle de riddle. And off we went."

"Pay your rent, did you, Murph?"

"Didn't I, though? Bastards must've thought I was some kind of a ship passing in the bleeding night, mustn't they? Made me pay up front. Bleeding cutthroats."

"Now tell me about London, Murph. And young Arthur."

"Mind, Detective Inspector, sir, I'm not saying anything against my own flesh and blood."

"Save it, Murph. Give that load of cock to the next social worker you see, but not me. You'd shop your own mother and father for a deal and we both know it, so shut your goddam bunghole of a face unless you are going to tell me what I want to know. And if you don't I will break your balls and make you eat them, you shit."

"Aw."

"Where can we find Freddy?"

162

"I swear to God, Inspector, I dunno. You got to get him, though." His eyes were open in the most genuine fear he had shown. "He tried to bite my cock off. I'll show you if—"

"Keep you filthy pud to yourself," Hooker roared at him. "I don't care if he did bite it off, I don't want to see it."

"He bit the heads off two pigeons," the man in the bed said almost casually. "In Hyde Park. I knew he wasn't right then. Two live pigeons, just like that. That scared me, I can tell you."

"So you two decided to get married. Jesus Christ."

I wasn't sure if Hooker was swearing or praying. I was praying. It went on. Like squeezing pus.

At the end of an hour that seemed like four, Hooker had it all out of him but the details. The job to steal a trunkload of books, the trip to Massachusetts, the second try in Ottery, and Freddy going berserk in the kitchen with the knife.

It was Freddy's idea in Oldhampton to steal the model ship out of the first trunk. He had a thing about ships, had a full-rigged sailing vessel tattooed on his back. Murph had smashed it in the back of the van rather than have them carrying a piece of evidence under their arms all the way back to England.

And it had been Freddy's idea to steal the red boat when they saw it in Gus's house. Then, when they heard the baby cry and found him in the cradle in the living room, it had been Freddy's inspiration to put him in the boat and set him floating down the stream.

"Right out to fucking sea he'll go, Murph," Freddy had laughed, "all the way to fucking China, like Moses in the bulrushes."

Then, because he had sunk into the mud of the stream bank up to his ankles, Freddy had got angry and lifted the boat with the baby in it over his head and hurled it into the mud with all his strength.

Then they had gone back, taken the trunk, loaded it into the van, and driven away. "I do like a Ford," Murph said to me moronically. "Green if I can get it."

I was drenched with sweat, and my stomach was churning

with nausea. The abject wreckage of the man in the bed, covered with his own blood, and the hellish stink everywhere, and the knowledge of what had happened in Gus's house was literally making my knees buckle. I leaned against the wall hard for support and prayed. Jesus Christ. Jesus Christ.

Hooker never relented, never backed off an inch.

"Where did you take it?"

"Left it in the van in a garridge in Exeter, locked. That's all. Arthur gave us an old Volvo to drive off in. I ask you, a Volvo. We were supposed to get fifty quid each that night and fifty again later, but the bloody bugger never coughed one p. After all that. I been here since then, Hooker, you believe me, don't you? Take me in, Hooker, please. Take me in, but you tell them I never done the kid or the woman, and I never touched that baby, Hook, I swear to God."

Hawley gave him two minutes to put on pants and a shirt and took him out of that hellhole.

Storey stepped back from the door and shook his head. "Christ, the stink. How did you take that for an hour?"

Then he took a look at Hooker Hawley's face and didn't ask any more questions. Hooker was in torment, his eyes sunken and his mouth set so that his lips were almost invisible, the lines on his face etched deeper, as though he were gritting against mortal pain.

Outside on the sidewalk I let it go and vomited everything I had in me. No one said a word. Storey took the prisoner in his car, where another shadowed figure was sitting waiting. Jones simply nodded out his driving window and drove off.

Hooker and I got back into his car like two men who had been beaten by a mob, dragging ourselves. When he started to drive, his hands shook on the wheel. He sat there breathing slowly, his eyes shut. Then he started the car and drove off very carefully.

"That," he said. "That's what a cop does for a living."

We drove in silence. Then he said, "You feel ashamed, don't you?"

"Yes."

164

"Because you're human."

I said nothing. Then, "The glamour of evil."

"Yeah."

"That's what it says in the baptismal service. 'I reject the glamour of evil.' "

"Some don't."

19

"I'M SORRY I did that," Hooker said to me.

We were in my apartment having coffee. He took the cup from me and tasted it. "Nice change."

"Did what?"

"Took you along to nab Murph."

"I can't say I enjoyed it, but I'm not sorry you let me tag along. You could have got in big trouble doing that, couldn't you? Have you?"

He waved off the suggestion. "From Bobby? That twit? You saw him. All ass and teeth."

"Not the C.I.D. people?"

"Ach, no. No one knows who the hell you are, and as long as you go back into the woodwork you came out of, what do they care? The Yard thinks Marbury's mob had you in, and Marbury thinks Special Branch is running some kind of hands-across-the-sea dance with the Yanks, but they don't know if it's the CIA or the FBI."

He drank off too much of the scalding coffee and spat it back in the cup. "Jesus, that's hot."

"My Irish mother would say that's your guardian angel burning your tongue for lying to all those fine policemen."

"Sure. I run my own race, I decided that years ago. Break ten rules a month. Ninety-nine percent of it never gets noticed. There aren't enough people down there who know my job as well as I do, and none better."

"What happens with the one percent that gets noticed?"

"What happens with your one percent?"

"Mine gets passed over because no one wants to tangle with me. I've been around the college so long that I simply know more ways of skinning a cat than anyone else."

"There you are. No, it's no fear of that lot that makes me regret dragging you up to Soho with me." He rubbed his nose vigorously with one finger. "I think I got carried away. I wanted you to see for yourself. A load of self-dramatization."

"I can see that. It's still all right, though. I learned some things."

"Nothing you needed to. I won't mention it again. And don't expect to go on any more excursions, racing in squad cars through the darkened London night."

I knew he meant it, and I knew he really was deeply embarrassed that it had happened.

He asked me to tell him more about Francis Li and the notebooks.

It had been the dragon trunk full of the Commander's notebooks that Murph and the still at-large Freddy had taken from Gus's house.

Someone had hired the two thugs to steal them. Someone who had been in England to begin with, and had known— or thought he knew—that I was in Massachusetts and had the trunk in my possession.

When the burglary in Oldhampton had produced nothing but a trunkful of boy's souvenirs, the two had flown back to England.

Someone had called my house and got my address in England from Bradley Oakes after learning that I was not in America.

Almost immediately the Brown Cottage in Ottery St. Mary was vandalized by someone looking for something. We now knew from Murph that he and Freddy had done both break-ins, and that in both Freddy had taken something with him that caught his fancy, and Murph had taken it away from him and thrown it away. At the Brown Cottage it was a stamp-collecting book with some stamps showing sailing ships.

After the Brown Cottage had turned out not to be my residence in England, someone had bothered to trace me to Gus.

"That wouldn't have been such a difficult feat, after all," Hooker grunted, staring admiringly out over the water at a quarter-mile-long supertanker.

167

"No, I suppose not. Elementary police work, ask around here and there for the odd stranded American tourist."

"Ask that lad in the marked van, who was seen, no doubt, by a watching Mrs. Gilbert to give you a lift. A talkative, friendly lad, you say. Then ask the innkeeper, my host Will Hayhurst, and Bob's your uncle, he tells them that Mr. Van Duren mentioned you'd be staying down at his place. A good innkeeper would be able to tell them everything else you two said in addition. He did me. It wouldn't be jumping to much of a conclusion to miss the one extra step and think you're down in Raleigh's Gill in the new house."

And, of course, Gus had then promptly received a phone call out of the Chinese blue from Francis.

Francis.

Obsessed Francis. Francis the acolyte of the Commander. Francis who would move heaven and earth to get his hands on the formula he believed existed. Francis who talked about the death of millions, but who would not or could not speak of the death of one. Francis the chess master.

Francis, Francis, Francis.

Logic without the saving grace of reason equals obsession. Obsession equals madness. But obsession courted, obsession accepted in trade for one's soul, for the sole purpose of gaining power, that was not madness, but evil.

Shortly thereafter I had met Francis in London—by chance?—and he and Gus and I had had our reunion at the Legation Hotel.

What had we talked about? Everything under the sun, east and west. Including a joking request from Gus that I finally take that goddam ton of stuff in the dragon trunk off his hands because it was taking up half his study.

Francis had come to see me in Raleighston, pressing me for the notebooks. Or at least for the formula, which he apparently believed was in the final notebook. He was unable or unwilling to accept my story that I had been with my father when he handed his so-called formula over to Sir Edmund in the Tartar City early in 1937, just before the Japanese crossed the Marco Polo Bridge and started what turned out to be World War II.

If Sir Edmund had the formula, it would either have been with the papers he took with him to the old Austrian Legation, where he lived after the Japanese burned his house in 1939—papers he subsequently had stored in the cellar of St. Michael's Hospital in the French Legation area, where he died—or in the papers stolen by the Japanese.

All of the papers taken by the Japanese had been moved to Manchukuo, according to Francis, and then taken from there after the war by the Russians. They in turn had shipped them all back to Moscow, where Francis says he had seen the great dictionary and the memoirs of Li Lien-ying.

But for him the proof that the Commander's scientific notebook was not in Moscow was the history of Russia's efforts to arrive at a forecasting and management formula for meteorological experimentation.

Francis thought that the documented period of freak weather that had ruined agriculture in a dozen northern hemisphere nations while Russia had enjoyed ideal growing weather was plenty of evidence that Russia had been experimenting with weather control. The fact that in the sixth year of the cycle Russia herself had suffered disastrous storms and a winter of a severity unprecedented even there, convinced him that the experiment had gone berserk, so that the Soviets had abruptly stopped whatever they were doing. He compared it to a nation having nuclear weapons but being unable to predict when they would go off—a situation so unstable that it effectively neutralized any advantage the weapons gave them.

But he was positive that the Russians were close, perhaps were in the ultimate phase of their weather management program. And he was sure that China was to be the great laboratory in which the Russians planned to conduct their next experiment. He swore that Chinese intelligence had documents to prove that.

All of it was perfectly believable to me, except the most important detail. I could not in a million years accept the reality of Francis's assessment of my father's "formula" as some meteorological equivalent of $E = MC^2$.

"Does it make any difference?" Hooker asked me.

We were both standing at my bay window now, watching the supertanker move along the horizon, taking turns with my Zeiss 10 × 50 binoculars.

"Jesus, those are beautiful glasses. Who did you get them off, a Nazi general?" he said, handing them back.

"Gift. What do you mean, any difference? Isn't that the whole difference?"

"Not essentially, no. Imagine I'm a loony. I'm having hallucinations. I look out this window, and I see a battleship sailing straight at me. It comes up on the beach and aims all its guns right at this window. I'm in the greatest possible danger, so I scream and want to run. But you, normal, healthy you, you don't see any battleship. Because there isn't any. I'm having hallucinations. To me they're real. So when you try to stop me running away, I pitch you out the window and run like hell."

"Ah. The existential reality for you *is* the battleship."

"I prefer the way I said it. Give me those glasses if you aren't going to use them."

"It doesn't make any difference, does it, whether there is a battleship out there or not?"

"Not to me it doesn't. Same as pink elephants to a bloke with the D.T.'s. Or voices from God to some poor bird dying of thirst in the desert. My reality is *that.*"

"I could never convince Francis in a million years that the formula doesn't exist or that it's simply gibberish produced by a wacky amateur, could I?"

"You could not. Nor all the king's horses and all the king's men. It's his holy grail or lost valley of emeralds or whatever you want to call it. He'll die to get it, will your Francis, and I think he will kill to get it. Has."

The logic was there, but I had fought accepting the conclusion it dictated and I was still doing so. Francis was, like my own father, a man obsessed, but was he also capable of hiring thugs who would murder to carry out his orders?

"It's Occam's razor, isn't it?"

"What is?" He looked at me strangely.

"A principle of philosophical logic. William of Occam

170

said that the right answer would always be the simplest one consistent with all the facts."

"Good man. He's right."

"But what if we don't know all the facts?"

"Room for doubt still exists, I'll admit that."

"Granted Murph matches the description, and there was no Russian spy loose in Oldhampton. And granted Murph and Freddy are the killers who stole the trunk. Is it absolutely out of the question that while Francis was beavering away trying to *talk* me out of the formula he thought I had, someone else was trying to beat him to it by stealing the formula?"

"No, it's not absolutely out of the question." He seemed reluctant to follow this turn in the speculation, but Hooker was an honest man.

"Odd thing came up with Jones the other day when we were talking about this and that. Marbury's man, you recall, the one who can't speak Chinese." A wintry grin. "The Prime Minister, no less, was raising hell about a question in Parliament she hadn't expected, from some pillar of the British Legion. Fellow wanted to know in so many words. why in bloody hell it was possible for Russian seaman—most of them probably trained espionage agents, in his view—to enter England at any port and go any damn where they pleased?"

I was surprised. "Can they? I thought the restrictions were pretty tight, as they are at home."

"Tight on the ones carrying diplomatic passports, yes. But it's true. There's a loophole in the law the Russians could drive a lorry through if they want to, and apparently they have. The buggers have been seen from Exmouth to Newcastle, going about free as you please, cameras and all, just a lot of happy tourists."

"Then it is conceivable—just conceivable, mind you— that some Russian agent or group is actually the direction behind the thefts."

"And the murder," he added drily. "Yes. It's conceivable. I suppose my trouble might be that I've had too much ex-

171

perience with our version of your McCarthyites, wild-eyed patriots who've seen a Russian behind every British failure since Bevan."

"Is Jones the one responsible for investigating that possibility?"

"Fear not, Marbury loves the Russian idea. Call from the P.M.? Questions in Parliament? The trumpet of bloodless battle for Dennis Darling."

"And meanwhile?"

"Meanwhile I have three detective sergeants and four detective constables opening and searching every 'garridge' in Exeter. Murph said they were met on New Bridge Street by a brown Ford Escort and led to the place. No address. He says he was never in Exeter before and didn't know where he was once he got in. He thinks, the ignorant turd, that it was across on the north side of the city, but he's not sure. And neither is he sure it was an actual garage. A storage shed perhaps, or an abandoned factory floor. Freddy was driving and he was drinking a pint of whisky to get over the shakes, according to him."

"Do you think Freddy will know?"

"We'll have to see when we have our hands on him, won't we? Half the Devon and Cornwall force is looking for him, but he's probably back in London, too. The Yard knows him well enough. A full-rigged ship tattoo is pretty fair identifying marks. Storey is turning over his regular places. Takes time, it does, in that place. And Arthur, of course, has disappeared from God's green earth."

"I sound like an amateur twit, I know, but I'd have thought Storey's men would have grabbed brother Arthur immediately."

"If not sooner." He shrugged eloquently. "No, you had the right thought. But after the row we made sweating the poison out of Murph, Arthur was probably called by whoever heard it and gone away on holiday before we had his big brother in the car."

"The van and the trunk might be long gone."

"Again, possible. Not likely, though. After Freddy got

through spilling blood all over this simple job, nobody in his right mind is going to go near that van."

"What would somebody not quite in his right mind do, do you think, if he thought the van was about to be discovered? If, mind you, he also thought the trunk really did contain, say, the Holy Grail?"

"Francis?" He cocked his right eyebrow and whistled a silent, short tune. "Francis might just make a bold, silly move and try to get it out first."

20

MY IMAGE OF Chelsea—swinging Chelsea of the maisonettes and wildly fashionable mews—was not the Chelsea of St. Leonard's Terrace, SW 3.

Edwina's extra residence was a period house with a park in front of it and a walled rear garden tended to flower-show perfection. There were two first-floor wings, and room to spare upstairs.

Edwina collected clocks. That explained all the family references to them. Not ordinary clocks or traveling clocks, but Sotheby and Christie's pieces, Victoria and Albert pieces. She and I visited them.

In the foyer, facing one another, were two, a walnut longcase—I acquired the term from my guide—by Daniel Quare, seven and a half feet high, and an even older ebonized longcase clock by William Clement, which Edwina told me was dated 1685. In the drawing room entrance was a floral marquetry clock just seven feet tall by Robert Harris, every inch of its gilt bordered case covered with designs of flowers, vases, and birds. There were at least three table clocks—to an amateur the collection quickly became a blur of unbelievable antiques, immensely valuable—a rare miniature spring Thomas Tompion less than ten inches high, and a Brighton Pavilion skeleton clock, the only note of whimsey in the collection. Sue had apparently said to Edwina that I was interested in clocks and had some, and that was all she needed to lay down a withering barrage of insider's special detail. I didn't know how I'd tell her if she asked that my "collection" consisted of a 1910 Seth Thomas from a schoolhouse torn down in Hadley and a bar clock from Cambridge graduate-school days with Mickey Mouse pointing to the time.

While she was delaying me with her collection, Sue and Gus, I gathered, were explaining once again why I was invited to Sue's mother, Lady Fox, who saw no reason why outsiders, even godfathers, should be there. Publicity had left her ill and bitter, willing to believe that the presence of anyone not a member of the family added to the sensationalism and cheap notoriety they had been through.

Sue's parents were with her and Gus in the drawing room when I entered. Lord Fox was a pear-shaped man with a drooping white moustache. He looked like a pudding, but he shook hands like a coal miner.

Her mother, a frail woman with white hair and eyes sunken into brown pools, a slash of thin scarlet lipstick dramatizing the set of her face, lifted a thin hand and blinked forlornly.

I said hello again to Donald, the clerical brother. It was a mournful occasion, since we were all meeting to attend the burial service for Richard, and no one made any false effort to lighten the hour.

The minutes each weighed a solemn ton while we sat and accepted tea from a servant and drank it and made quiet small talk about moving back to London and prepared ourselves to be driven to the church in Lord Fox's Rolls Royces.

Sue had been determined that Richard would not be buried back in Ottery. She said flatly that she would never go there again, and that is what was responsible for today's burial service in London.

The church was St. Pancras, Younger, by Victoria Grove, a tiny, unsteepled, gray stone building which seemed ancient and had some family association. The Fox family had at least two family members buried and memorialized there, and I gathered from an oblique reference Sue's mother made about the Vicar's knowing which side his bread was buttered on that she, at least, felt certain proprietary privileges were theirs automatically. Perhaps they supported the virtually unattended church, and that still does carry its privileges.

There, on a day of drizzling rain, in a corner of St. Pancras, Younger, churchyard, we said the ritual prayers together. Father Donald read the bold words of St. Paul to the Corinthians, mocking death's empty and temporal victory, and we buried the heartbreakingly small coffin and body of Richard Arthur Van Duren, servant of God, toward the end of what would have been the sixth week of his life on earth.

21

FRANCIS CALLED ME Friday about noon and asked me to meet him in Exeter.

"Just two old chums meeting for a fine talk, yes, and perhaps to say a sad good-bye, Neil. My government is not pleased with the attitude of Oxford University in the matter of the Backhouse manuscripts, and they would Li Chen please to come home and explain all this to them." The familiar giggle was still working.

"Why Exeter? Why don't you come down here and talk?"

"Oh, Neil, I am grieved. Are you being devious? Are you having your nice flat bugged by Marbury's commandoes and all that? Perhaps they have done it and you do not even know, eh? No, no, dear Neil. Come to Exeter, a marvelous, historical city, almost as old as Shanghai, and we will walk around the great cathedral if you wish and talk of shoes and ships and sealing wax, I believe."

I remembered that the van with the trunk in it had been left in Exeter by Murph and Freddy.

"Very well, Francis. I shall meet you in the library there."

"In the public library? How odd."

"No. The Cathedral library. It happens to be one of the few places I know in Exeter where very few people go. One of the oldest books in English is there, an Anglo-Saxon book, and a few scholars go there to see it. I shall show you the Domesday Book, too."

"That sounds a bit hair-raising, doesn't it, the Domesday Book? Where is this quiet library you like so much?"

I explained how to get into the Bishop's Palace behind the Cathedral and where the library is on the second floor.

"You mean the first floor, do you not, Neil? I think I much prefer the British designation. Ground floor, then first floor. The Bishop's Palace, my, how very Renaissance and decadent that sounds. I shall feel more like Francis Borgia than Francis Li."

"I shall have to take a bus. The library is open 'til five; I shall try to be there between four-thirty and five."

"Just one more thing, old chum, Neil. Do not, I beg you, bring your new chum, Inspector Hawley, with you. Let this be just a meeting between old friends for a final chat, eh?"

As soon as I hung up I tried to reach Hawley in Exmouth, in Raleigh's Gill, and in Exeter itself. No one seemed to know where the independent-minded inspector could be found, although I did find that he was due to meet with his search teams in Exeter at the end of their afternoon shift.

I almost felt reprieved. I had made the effort to find him, and now I would go alone and find out what was there and bring whatever influence argument could exert to bear on Francis. I had the vague sense that I was re-enacting Hooker's self-dramatization up in London, but perhaps nothing else would assuage the bitter feelings of guilt plaguing me. All this had happened because of something of mine, a trunk full of nonsense that had become someone else's Holy Grail, as Hooker had put it. I didn't know just what my responsibility was, but I knew I had one.

So I went to Exeter on the three-thirty bus in a driving rain. One pound seventy, round trip. I assumed it would be a round trip; I certainly hoped so.

Francis was waiting for me at the head of the stairs leading from the lower hall up to the Cathedral library. It was quarter of five, and the magnificent clock on the landing, which even Edwina would have coveted, was just singing the quarter hour in deep, melodious strokes as I ascended to greet him.

He was obviously in a fever of excitement. He looked brilliant-eyed and flushed, like a man on drugs. But I knew that Francis had said he would never touch drugs, and that his appearance could only be the effects of intense emotional stimulation.

He giggled richly and shook my hand with both of his, like a professional greeter. I had got soaked on my walk over in the rain from the bus station, and he helped me remove my coat and shake it out a little before going into the library.

"It looks so formidable in there, Neil," he whispered over my shoulder, "that I wanted to wait for you. If the books were in Chinese I would not mind, but I did not want to look like a very big fool reading Anglo-Saxon upside down or anything silly-buggers like that."

"Sorry if I kept you waiting, Francis. Come in, I do want to show you these splendid old books. Books like these have been my adult life. Look, how white and fresh the paper is. I have bought books newly published in the last ten years, and the paper is already yellowing, and . . . but of course, you people invented paper. I am talking to a Greek about philosophy."

We were both nervous. I wanted that in him. I wanted him so anxious to get on with it that he became careless. I showed him the minor marvels under glass to the right in the narrow room, then turned him so that he could see and appreciate The Exeter Book and The Domesday Book of Devon. I read to him from the double page reporting the census of the lands and holdings of the Baldwins in Wessex.

Throughout my boring exposition of what we were seeing —thank God there were no other visitors—he was a model student, patient and attentive. Then, suddenly the bubble of his thin patience burst and he hissed at me.

"I think I have seen all that I wish to see of these truly remarkable treasures, Neil. But now, since it does not appear that you are being tailed—is that the American idiom?—by any of Inspector Hooker Hawley's minions, I think I shall now take you with me and show you the equally remarkable Priory of St. Austin, not very far from here."

He giggled and hiccupped. He really was excited. I knew now where we were going.

"Fine. But Francis, it would be considered the worst possible form to leave without signing the guest book. Kings and queens have signed it. The royal family."

"I say, the royal family? I should like to add my name to it before we leave, surely."

179

We had approached the desk of the librarian, where my graduate student friend, Thomas Wall, was discreetly working away at his filing. I gestured theatrically to the open guest book on the desk and said in a loud voice: "Pay no attention to me and read what I write." I took care to say it in Latin, and I did not look at Thomas Wall.

"What is that?" Francis said, picking up the pen to write his name and comment. "Aha, a Swedish count was here yesterday. That is something, at least."

"What I said was, 'Here is the book in which kings have written.' Do add an original comment of your own. One is expected to."

He wrote swiftly in Chinese, "The work of peace is done by scholars," and signed it in Chinese characters.

I took the pen. "Western scholars, you understand, are still expected to be literate in Latin, especially here. I always have the damndest time, frankly, thinking of Virgil or Horace at these moments. Oh, dear, I suppose I'll have to fall back on Cicero." I wrote, in Latin: "At the benedictine monastery of saint augustine call inspector holly immediately isca five two one nine one."

"There. A boring bit of Cicero on the need for study: 'In books we are both close to the human heart and safe from its dangers.'" I was rather proud of *ilex* for holly for Hawley. I still didn't dare look at young Wall.

"And now it is my turn to guide the tour, eh? Come, come, my car is parked just outside, we will not let you get wetted again."

I put my coat over my shoulders and we trotted down the staircase.

"I am parked in a space marked Reserved For Diocesan House Staff," he giggled. "Do you think they will forgive me my trespasses, eh?"

Before we went out into the parking area, Francis stopped in the downstairs hall and took a newspaper from his pocket.

"As you can see, Neil, a copy of today's *Guardian*. An admirable, progressive paper for England. Let me show you just one small piece in *The Guardian*. On page twenty-one, at the bottom, what they call a filler. You see, I have it circled."

He held it out to me to read. It was just what he said, a filler. Ten lines from Reuters, quoting the New China News Agency, dateline Peking.

> A 400-square mile hollow has developed beneath Peking because of excessive use of underground water combined with the worst drought in 32 years. The cavity beneath the capital and its outskirts was created when the water table dropped by two or three yards.

"Isn't it amusing how they headline that little item, eh? 'Hollow Feeling.' How droll. The funny Chinese are about to lose their greatest city. If it were London so threatened, or Paris, do you suppose *The Guardian* would engage in these clever ironies? And on page twenty-one? Do they realize that Peking faces, in effect, a cataclysmic earthquake? Then must we assume that they do not care?"

I handed him back his paper. "Surely it is the Chinese, Francis, who are draining off the water supply, not the Russians."

"Oh, yes. But why, Neil? That is the point. Did you miss this phrase: 'worst drought in thirty-two years'? I think the Russians have begun, Neil." He was hoarse with the intensity of his whispering.

"If they have, then they must now have the formula you have been trying to find in England. And if that is so, then who else but you could have been directing these thefts and crimes which became murders, Francis?"

He stared at me and then shrugged as if a negligible secret had been revealed. The surprise he had planned was tarnished, perhaps, but not entirely spoiled.

"That does not matter. If the Russians have developed the formula for themselves, it is even more imperative, is it not, for the Chinese people to find the original formula?"

He still spoke with the obsessive's unshakable conviction.

We dashed to his car, a scarlet Leyland Minivan, through the downpour.

St. Austin's Priory, set along the west edge of Bartholomew Street, had been built originally about 1150. It had been attacked, disestablished, fortified, restored, and burnt. Only the west range survived complete now, the south wing having been demolished by the city itself after the bombings of 1942 had weakened the structure beyond tolerance. It overlooked the deep Longbrook Valley, and had been incorporated at one time into the city wall because of that natural defensive placement.

Within, it was a warren of monk's cells and studies and halls, connected and interconnected by precipitous, worn stone stairways. For the past year it had been taken off the tour lists so that extensive repairs could be made to its sagging roof and walls. Fundraising was slow—even Exeter Cathedral, by far the most popular tourist site in the city, was having a struggle to raise funds to rebuild its famous west front.

I had visited the Priory hurriedly, just to say that I had walked part way round it, on the same day that Tom Wall and I had lunched together and then walked back along Bartholomew Terrace for the view of the river.

Whether it was his manic state or natural habit, Francis drove like a Grand Prix contestant, accelerating out of the Palace yard and speeding through the twisting narrow streets below the High, never letting up his chattering and arguing. He was not simply obsessed, he was on fire with the urgency of his conviction. He spun recklessly around corners, peering through the sluicing windshield wipers, but never hesitating.

We braked with shocking abruptness beside the high wall of the Priory. It looked black and forbidding in the rain. Francis backed and angled the car onto the thick plank gangway that spanned a shallow ditch between the road and the building. Then he hopped nimbly out and went the rest of the way up the short bridge, calling back, "Sit yourself there and I shall open the doors, Neil."

With only the car's headlights for illumination, he opened a padlock from the hasp holding the big double sliding doors shut and pushed them back. They must have been counterweighted, because they moved easily for him.

He ducked back into the Minivan. "And now, Neil, you will want to see your old trunk with the golden dragon, eh? And the notebooks of the Commander for which you say so dramatically Francis has become a murderer? I shall show you."

We drove slowly over the planked way. "Do not worry, this is quite safe. I have been over it many times." We drove through the double doors and onto the floor of what appeared to be an immense rectangular barn. Directly ahead of us, head on, was the green Ford van.

"See, see, here it is. Half the police in England are looking for it, and here it sits, receiving sanctuary, so to speak, from this ancient church."

He whipped the Leyland around and parked it parallel with the Ford, facing the street. He jumped out and almost pranced gleefully over to the green van, and threw open the rear doors. Then he ran to the double doors and slid them shut and threw the light switch on the wall.

Now I got out of the car and I could see the old black trunk with the golden dragon on it, the object of all his scheming and evil actions. He applauded as if a marvelous trick had come to its climax.

"*Voilà*, Neil, my old chum. And now Li Chen, who has been so unfairly criticized for being unable to persuade Oxford University to relinquish the books of Sir Edmund, will again be a person of considerable esteem when he returns to Peking. Because he will have in his hands the formula of the Commander."

The two of us stood there looking at that miserable tin trunk with its cheap, garish decoration.

"And now I make you an offer. Come, share a last drink with me in the refectory of this house of hospitality, where I have wine and bread waiting. We shall talk. We shall debate, if you wish. Argue. Discuss. And the superior debater will take the trunk, eh? You see for yourself, the doors are unlocked."

He pointed to the opposite wall, where a similar pair of double doors were secured by having a six-foot-long two-by-four nailed across them. "Not those. That way there is only scaffolding. All tick-tock, double lock there. Will you join me for the challenge debate? The question will be, who should take the trunk home with him, eh?" His laugh was a preposterous cackle.

"I really won't take no for an answer. I have planned this oh so carefully, do not disappoint me." His eyes were dilated and dancing with mischief.

"I say, do help me shift this terribly heavy trunk into my car, will you? There's a good chap."

There was literally nothing I could do but stay with him, mad as he was. If I left, he would drive away. It was still possible that I might reach him, through the baffling defenses he had erected against reason. He had once been my friend, and my father had admired him like another son.

My skin crawling, I lifted one end of the trunk and helped him move it.

"Will you answer all my questions, Francis, if I stay here and have this so-called debate with you?"

"Will I not? But of course, of course." He slammed the trunk into the Leyland and closed the door. "All questions will be answered, just follow Li Chen. I will get the lights as we go. All electric now for the tourists, you see."

He seemed to have no difficulty finding the switches that lit our way ahead, and extinguished the lights behind us as we went. My feet seemed to weigh a ton each, but I went after him. Only where he went was there light, and only at the end would there be any hope of reasoning with him and getting him, if he required it, to accept medical help through me. In all charity, the men he had hired to steal for him had made him an accessory to murder, but I did not know that inside himself he wasn't as scared as I was.

He called back with the same hysterical cheerfulness as he twisted and turned through the stone corkscrew stairways. "Follow Father Francis. Even I get confused in this holy maze sometimes. I suppose even these old monks who lived here a lifetime did, too, eh?"

After five doors and half a dozen short, curving stairs of

three or four steps each, the stone worn to a width of only inches on most of them, we entered another large space and Francis turned on the lights. It was a medieval kitchen and refectory. An enormous oak table set with a few stools and one thick chair was stretched across the room in front of a ten-foot fireplace. This had obviously been the place where meals were prepared for the whole community, and three long spits with two-man handles and a variety of bake ovens and huge iron pots were visible inside the work area. The table was incongruously set with paper plates and picnic foods. A loaf of Mother's Pride white sliced bread, a small jar of pickles, and a package of salami were laid out with a bottle of Peter Dominic's white plonk.

It was certainly cold enough in the underground room to keep food indefinitely.

Francis unscrewed the cap from the wine bottle with a flourish. "Poor stuff, but we monastics must look to our vow of poverty, eh? You know, I'm sure, Neil, that the reason we keep wine at fifty-one degrees is that it was the room temperature in a well-heated castle. I think the monks got used to having their wine about five or six degrees cooler, eh?" He giggled and handed me a paper cup of wine.

"To friendship. And to Peking, our old home. And, oh yes, to our debate. I have always wanted to debate with a college professor from the west. A kind of intellectual table tennis, ping-pong, as you call it; we Chinese are very competitive that way."

"Francis, I want you to come with me to the police. If you tell them now how it all happened, where this Freddy is, and how the whole thing got out of control, I'm absolutely sure that it can be resolved."

"Resolved, Neil? Resolved?" He cocked his head and stared at me roguishly. "There is nothing to resolve. What on earth can you be talking about? In any event, do remember that I have complete diplomatic immunity for myself. This poor person is quite safe."

He lifted his finger. "But it is the trunk and its contents which we must guard, eh? They, sadly, have no immunity, and I alone am responsible for getting them out of perfidious Albion and safely back to the Middle Kingdom."

I pleaded with him again. We argued quietly, like a couple of old friends in a pub arguing whether one of them should stop drinking and come home. My arguments were all reasons, his were all mockery.

"Let me quote something to you, Neil." He began without waiting for my assent and without having to summon the words to mind. " 'The great drama of humanity is this: man's task is to finish creation, by completing and bettering it, by causing order to increase. That is the human vocation.' " He was standing now, as if pronouncing a valedictory.

" 'That is the human vocation, the dignity of co-creator. Instead, either voluntarily or involuntarily, he fosters the growth of disorder. We live not in an absurd world, but a world made absurd by human stupidity and sin. History therefore is an inextricable'—an *inextricable*—'tangle of good and evil.' "

He paused with his head cocked, as if savoring the words.

I knew what he was quoting, as he knew I would. He and Gus and I had all discussed our separate discoveries of Pierre Chardin and our regard for him that night of our reunion. It was one of the coincidences we had rejoiced in, made more personal by the fact that Chardin, the old Jesuit, had lived in Peking too. Had, in fact, been the discoverer of China's oldest human skeletal evidence, Peking Man.

"Pierre Teilhard de Chardin."

"Yes. Chardin. The great genius the Jesuits tried to silence because his thoughts were unwelcome to their Italian ears. Another old Peking hand, eh?"

"He was talking about man's vocation under God when he wrote that."

"Oh yes. If my people, who, you must surely recall, had no word at all in classical Chinese for what your people called 'God,' and if we prefer to say 'History,' what is the harm?"

186

"*Tin shoo po yaw*. God bless you."

"Ah, Our Gang's ancient password. Our shibboleth, eh? But it is not 'God,' is it? It is *t'ien*, a word much closer in meaning to Natural Law or Logos. The Chinese are closer to the Greeks than to the Jews."

"Nevertheless, you are perverting Chardin's thought."

"I am perverting it? So you say. But I think that the Jesuits and the Vatican, both of whom condemned him, might think I had it precisely. Father Chardin, like us, Neil, lived in China, not in Paris or Rome. He liberated himself from his European cultural prejudices and he saw the truth. Our vocation is to make order."

"My godchild is dead."

"Mourn him, then. It is only human."

"Your people killed him."

"Or your people, which? To protect a handful of mathematical calculations, a box of old books."

"No," I shouted at him, furious. "Not us, you."

"How many dead children did you mourn for in the streets of Peking in the years you lived there, Neil? Were there five thousand every year? And how many in Hiroshima, and in Vietnam? Was your godchild an elite of one who somehow deserved to live forever? Was he better than all those Chinese children and Japanese and Vietnamese children?"

"Unless I believe that every child is an elite of one innocent person, and refuse to play your games of murder justified by an appeal to a heaven that is really a hell, I am no better than you. And you and your argument from some imaginary God of History who is not himself a person but some blind force are vomit, the sickness of history, not its cure. You create cancer and you call it order. Yes, there is terrible stupidity, and there is also deliberate sin, and they are not the same, goddam you, Francis."

He stood and screamed back at me, cursing my smugness and my comfortable democratic individualism. We both stood, shouting and spitting like two madmen at one another. My throat was torn with shouting and he grew hoarse with the force of his anger, hurling it at me like a weapon, as though words could kill.

God knows how long we went on. Suddenly it was silent between us, and we hung exhausted across the table, staring blankly at each other. He poured out the last of the wine into the two cups and we drank it without saying any more. I was trembling and weak with the draining away of my rage.

"Well," Francis said at last, panting like an exhausted racer, "I have not converted you and you have not converted me. Therefore I must go, and you must stay here."

"What are you talking about? I'm not going to stay here, whatever you do."

He skipped to the stairway we had come by and stood on the first stair, swinging shut behind him a barred iron gate that stretched from the floor to the top of the doorway. He spoke through the grill.

"Yes, you must. I cannot let you walk away from here and alert those police friends of yours so that they can chase down my little van and take back the trunk from me, can I? Not after all I have had to endure to enjoy its possession."

I looked around me in every direction. It was a large prison, but it was a prison.

"You have some bread there, and some meat. Perhaps enough for a week if you are frugal, Neil. And perhaps by then a workman or the ghost of some old Benedictine brother will come wandering down here and release you. If not, well, this is holy ground, is it not, and a good place to meditate on death while you die. Your friend John Donne, the priest who was in love with death, will be a comfort to you, I am sure."

"Francis, don't do this. Don't add murder to the things you have done."

"It is an addition of one, merely, Neil. Over in the west wing in a very tiny stone cell that was once the gateway to heaven for some holy brother, there is poor Freddy, whom you are looking for. I do not know if he is dead yet or not, but it does not matter. I dropped a sizable medieval stone on his head and dragged him there myself, oh, a good week ago. And in another cell nearby is Mr. so-called Young Arthur, who was employed in various unsavory enterprises by my cousin, Jimmy Dzu, and who acted, shall we say, as my honest broker in all this. Yes, Freddy and his dreadful companion were Arthur's agents and Arthur was mine. He has been my guest here since the day they drove the Ford van in from Ottery. He never left, you see. I'm very much afraid that I ran him down with that same van while I was parking it just so upstairs." He laughed and thumped the iron gate. "Actually, I had to chase him back and forth, round and round that great hall, which once was an armory, before I caught him. A weapon the old knights never dreamed of, eh? He was in a frightful panic when he heard of what had happened."

"I was told that Freddy left with the other man."

"So he did. But he got greedy, I suppose, our young Freddy, and he came skulking back later to see what he could steal. He was standing in a narrow stairway trying to puzzle out how to get through a small, locked oak door when I dropped the stone on him from the recess above. Then I had to lock him up for his own good, didn't I? Just what the English police would do if they could. Do you suppose they will give me a commendation, eh?"

He was almost dancing with glee behind the gateway.

"Good-bye, Neil, old chum. *Tin shoo po yaw* and all that."

He was gone. The lights in the great kitchen went out, and after a few seconds even the sound of his footsteps, scrabbling up the stairs, was lost in the recesses of the stone fortress.

The black was palpable, and cold. I sat on a stool holding onto the edge of the table to keep oriented, frightened and near despair. Breathing as slowly as I could, the sweat of fear freezing my body and making me shake, I tried to pray. The only words were those I had found myself mumbling before at the edge of terror, "Jesus Christ, Jesus Christ."

I tried to tell myself I was prepared to sit there in the

frigid dark for hours, but if I let myself think of the possibility that it might be days or even weeks, I wanted to scream for help. Sooner or later I knew that someone would come, but the present reality was terrifying.

I groped for my paper cup of wine and drank it to steady myself. I tried to remember where the fireplace was, exactly. There must be a flue. Would they have blocked it up years ago to keep out pests? Wouldn't it be better to sit tight here rather than to start blundering around in the dark among the brutal iron tools and bruising stones?

It was probably only a half hour later, but that space of time held the black weight of night, when Hooker's voice came from above me, and with it the light from a flashlight.

"Neil? Neil Kelly? You down there?"

The flashlight found me and stopped. I must have looked like a man found down a well, a white face frozen in disbelief, staring up. He held the light under his own chin. He looked like a gargoyle image of himself, peering down through a high grill.

"Be right down, then. Bastard locked you in, did he?"

The light disappeared, then gradually reappeared around the curve of the stairway. Then Hooker found the switch, and the room was fully lit again.

He looked at me wryly through the bars of the gateway. "Going in for the monastic lark, are you? Bread and cheese in the refectory before bed?"

He examined the padlock securing the gate and called back over his shoulder to John Pride. "Sergeant, get down here double-quick with the cutter, if you please. Kelly has locked himself in the larder and refuses to come out."

It took only a minute and I was free. I shook their hands as if we had not seen each other for years.

"Is he gone? Did the boy at the library get my message to you? What time is it? I'm completely disoriented."

"Hold on, hold on," Hooker said good-naturedly. We were all edging back up the winding stairs and back through several doors. Sergeant Pride was just narrow enough sideways. All the lights were on now, and I could hear some activity above us.

"Yes, your young friend at the library got your message to me right enough. Good lad, that. I've got four cars full up here. We got here and found the place shut tight and no lights and I said to John here, 'Is there another St. Austin's in Exeter, do you suppose?' "

He led the way out onto the stone-floored armory where the green van was still parked facing the wide-open double doors. The red Leyland Minivan was gone.

Hooker sighed. "And, yes, he's gone, has our Francis. Drove off like a shot."

"Dammit. Goddammit, he's escaped." My own anger and bitterness shocked me, the rage I felt in my own frustration. I clenched my fists helplessly.

"Right off the cliff wall, I'm very much afraid," Hooker said quietly. He led me by the arm to the open doors. "Don't rush out there after him unless you want a nasty bump. They've taken the restraining rail off the old gun parapet there, and it's a good fifty feet straight down if you go over. It certainly didn't do Francis's car a bit of good. That's it still smoldering down there on the rocks."

I stared out bewildered through the dark curtain of rain. Francis had driven out through the fortress wall, not the street doors. The spire of the Church of St. Michael loomed through the downpour directly across the narrow valley.

"But—" I whirled around. The opposite doors had a six-foot two-by-four nailed across them. The green Ford van was also parked facing this way.

"Sergeant Pride's idea, actually. Devious bugger is our John Pride. Used to be a student guide here until he got too wide for it. We got here and found this setup, with both cars facing back that way, toward the street, of course. I sent six men tiptoeing through this old chamber of horrors to see what was going on, and one of them found you and Francis having a rare old set-to down there in the kitchen. Sergeant Jenkins says you were going at it first in English, then in Chinese, then back in English. So fascinating, he said, that he could hardly tear himself away and report back.

"Meanwhile John and I simply took the barrier off those doors and nailed it across the others leading to the street.

You could fire off a cannon in here and never be heard. Then our John just reversed the two vans and left them facing the unlocked doors. Francis shoved them open with never a thought for the traffic regulations and roared off."

"You let him drive off the wall?"

"We couldn't stop him, could we? The man had diplomatic immunity. Burned to a crisp, though, despite that. After your old trunk landed on the back of his head and crushed that a bit. Popped the trunk open, so whatever was in it has been burned to cinders, too. A right mess."

The police photographers and forensic crew were going about their tasks in the usual bored fashion. A constable reported that he had found two bodies locked in cells in the lower west wing, both with crushed heads.

Hooker took my arm. "Let's go have a drink. Sergeant Pride, take over this lot, will you? And take down that piece of timber someone nailed over the doors to keep out the news people. I think that's no longer necessary."

I went with him in a daze, which he kept right on talking through as we drove out. "A drink of real whisky is what you need, not that terrible rotgut out of a paper cup. This round is on Inspector Ilex. I like that, more class than Hooker, somehow. I wonder if I can get John Pride to call me Inspector Ilex."

22

HOOKER AND I entered my apartment and I fell into the sofa gratefully. Despite the long ride from Exeter, and Hooker's calming, casual conversation about how the police would proceed methodically to clean up this bloody and disastrous case, I was still tense and shaking. College professors might encounter violence of that magnitude in a lifetime, even more than once, but they are neither constitutionally nor professionally prepared to absorb the effects and still function.

He poured us both a stiff Irish whisky from my small store of bottles, as though he were the host and Kelly the guest.

"Will you stay here now, Neil?" He sipped his drink appreciatively, one eyebrow up.

"Never. The book is shot. Hopeless. In a way I know more about what I want to say—John Donne's idea of death has never seemed so vivid and real to me as it is now. But I think I don't care enough to try.

"Ironic, isn't it? The saints have spoken about it for millenia, but you have to brush up against it yourself to understand."

"Understand what, that we all have to die?"

"No. We know that much earlier. No, not that we have to die, but what death is, what the value of anything we do is. It's nothing, isn't it? Either God puts a value on it or it's worth exactly nothing. Whether we compose *The Elegies* or *Lear*, or the *Fifth Symphony* or paint *The Last Supper*. *Sub specie aeternitatis*, as my catechism used to say, from God's point of view it is all equally pathetic with a child's dabs or a student's essay. Unless God values it for its moral significance, there is no worth in it at all, neither life nor death."

Hooker didn't say anything. Perhaps I was raving. He

picked up one of the Kyoto vases from my fireplace mantel and studied it.

"Is that good art or bad?"

"Both, and neither. God knows. The art is the virtue of the thing to be made, its ideal possible form, I suppose."

Hooker grunted. An academic's answer, no answer at all. He shook the bottle and held it to his ear. "What's in it?"

I laughed, remembering. "My God, I had forgotten. Not the famous missing formula, if you were thinking that. Something Pa sealed in there on my twelfth birthday. A reading from the *I Ching*. I had completely forgotten it was in there."

I took the vase from him and pried out the wax plug and turned the bottle upside down to shake out the small hard rolled cylinder of paper. It dropped into my hand. I unrolled it carefully and spread it on the table and read the Chinese characters.

I had been confirmed on my twelfth birthday, along with Gus and two or three other members of the Legation's child population, by the Chinese auxiliary bishop of Peking. Choosing a new middle name at Confirmation is a great event for Catholic boys and girls, and after tremendous deliberation and seventeen changes of mind, I had chosen Augustine. In honor of Gus I had taken the British form, Austin.

Pa had taken me to the old scholar after the cathedral ceremony, after the six of us, Kellys and Van Durens, had eaten a Chinese feast at the Gate of Heavenly Peace restaurant. The old scholar of the *I Ching* sat in a folding chair in the open-air market, with his inks and brushes on a tiny table in front of him. He had immense dignity, and the Commander greeted him with all the courtesy due to a scholar. He would have been as insulted to be called a fortune-teller as a Talmudic rabbi would be if you called him a puzzle addict.

He made me hold the yarrow sticks to cast my hexagram, watching me from beneath bushy white eyebrows, and writing down each line, yang or yin, bottom to top, until the double trigram was complete. Then he studied it and consulted his scroll copy of the *I Ching* and wrote down my reading with rapid black brush strokes.

"The *I Ching* is not just a book of oracles," Pa had said to my mother when she pshawed the idea of having a reading done for me on that day. "It is as old as the Book of Wisdom in the Old Testament, and the Chinese think that there are moments when the wisdom of the text and the events of your life can intersect, one throwing light on the other."

The old scholar handed the little text over to my father, who paid him and thanked him gravely, then did the meanest thing he had ever done to me: he read it and then rolled it up and put it in his pocket.

"I want you to read that on your twenty-first birthday, Neil, not now."

I begged and pleaded in vain. After the terrific buildup he had given it, I wanted to see that reading then, on the spot. It was my reading, wasn't it? I was the one who got confirmed, wasn't I? What kind of a mean guy was he, anyway? Didn't Ma think he should show it to me right then, huh, didn't she? She did, but that didn't cut any ice either.

He put the little scroll into one of the bottles on our mantlepiece when we got home and sealed it in with wax. My practical mother said, "Well, I won't have to wash that out every time the dust gets into it, will I? Might as well seal them both," and she did.

I tried to work up courage for weeks to carry out my plan to accidentally knock the bottle onto the floor and break it, forcing the issue. Then I forgot all about it. Until that moment when Hooker shook it and asked what was in it.

Now I held it open against the table and read the old man's classical brushwork.

"It's number thirty-six. Each *I Ching* reading is numbered. Thirty-six is called *Ming I*: 'the wounding of brightness.' " I read the text. " 'A man of dark nature is in a position of authority and brings harm to an able and wise man. First he climbed up to heaven, then he plunged to the depths of the earth.' That's it."

The eyebrow went up. "You think your dad couldn't know when you were twelve if you were the one or the other, the man of dark nature or the other? There was something bad in store for you either way, if he believed that."

"Parents can never know, can they? Will any great harm come to them, or from them, that we can't prevent?"

195

"True, by God. It's not what the kids think we sweat about, but it's true. I've always believed it was too bad, in some way, that we can't know, but I can see the worst would be knowing and knowing you can't prevent it."

He finished his drink and shook hands and left. That was the last time I saw Hooker Hawley.

I was called down to the Exeter headquarters of the Devon and Cornwall police the following day and asked to make a sworn deposition about what had happened. I told them what I knew of my personal knowledge, as instructed, and nothing else.

I garnered one additional fact, listening in on a conversation between a disgusted sergeant and a philosophical detective superintendent. The Chinese Embassy had refused to discuss Francis beyond issuing a statement regretting his action and explaining that he had already been ordered back to China for reasons of health.

When we were finished, and I had signed the statement, the officer in charge shook his head and marveled with me at the confusion that had caused Francis Li in his panic to drive out the wrong doorway when both were unbarred.

"Poetic justice, I suppose you could say, you being a professor of poetry and literature."

The awful cliché would do. I let it stand.

Then I went back to the Cathedral library and thanked Thomas Wall for the important favor of saving my life.

In the morning I packed my two bags and stood for the last time in the Raleigh's Cask and drank a pint. Then I got into a cab and began reversing my journey toward London, with the eventual goal of Scotland. It was as far as I could go from Devon and still be in Britain. Perhaps a hard hundred-mile walk through the Highlands and around the Hebrides would heal my harm.

THE BEST IN SUSPENSE

RICHARD HOYT

"Richard Hoyt is an expert writer."
—*The New York Times*

BESTSELLING BOOKS FROM TOR

MORE BESTSELLERS FROM TOR